I0621155

RED CARBON

D.J. GOODMAN

SEVERED PRESS
HOBART TASMANIA

RED CARBON

Copyright © 2015 D.J. Goodman
Copyright © 2015 by Severed Press

WWW.SEVEREDPRESS.COM

ISBN: 978-1-925342-17-8

"The challenge of the great spaces between the worlds is a stupendous one; but if we fail to meet it, the story of our race will be drawing to a close."

-Arthur C. Clarke

1

At 4:38 a.m. Rothschild Standard Time, Sandeep "Dip" Benegal opened up the v-mail he had received in the night and watched for four minutes as his brother-in-law filled him in on his sister's condition. When the video cut him off in mid-sentence, Dip figured it was just another hiccough in the notoriously crappy signal.

Although no one would realize it for another couple of hours, this was the first sign any of the employees in Mining Colony Miranda had that something had gone terribly wrong on Earth.

2

In her previous life, Annabeth Crick had been a fast food worker. She regularly put up with customers that thought she was lower than dog shit, dealt with managers who thought their different colored shirts made them superior despite the fact that she had a college education while they hadn't even finished high school, and would often come home at the end of the night with a thin coating of grease on her arms that she could scrape off with her nails. Even considering her profession now, she still considered it the worst job she'd ever had. But there were occasionally little annoyances in this job that made her long for a life of frying burgers. Such as right now, for example, when she had just finished putting her entire bulky environment suit on, including the helmet, before she looked over at the floor near her client's bed and realized she had forgotten to put on her underwear.

She unlatched the seals on her helmet and then undid her gloves. Despite the fact that there was nothing sexy about her suit or the hurried way she removed it, her client, Mikhail Svensson, grinned at her from his prone place on the bed as though she were repeating the striptease she had performed for him hours earlier.

"Decided to stay for a little overtime?" he asked. He gestured at the time clock on his wall. As much as she wanted to smack that look right off his face, she found herself grateful for the comment anyway, since her frilly panties weren't the only thing she had almost left without. Her tiny plastic time card was still in the clock. If she'd walked out without it and this ass had done something to it, then she wouldn't just lose her pay for last night but for all of last week as well. Time cards were like magic talismans in Miranda- they kept starvation and eviction away in the same way environment suits staved off the deadly elements.

Annabeth grabbed the timecard, put it in the carrying pocket on the left side of her suit, then continued pulling the suit off. It would have been much easier if she just put the underwear in the pocket as well, but nothing in the pockets received the same protection from the elements that it would inside the suit itself. She'd made the mistake of stuffing a bra that she had forgotten in a similar manner into the pocket once. The tiny bits of moisture on it had resulted in the bra freezing into a hard clump after she'd gone outside. Thawing it out and smoothing it back into a recognizable shape had taken longer than she was willing to deal with now.

Even as she continued to strip off the suit, Svensson seemed to lose interest in her. He extricated his pasty naked body from the sheets, stretched, then stood up and walked to his personal kitchen unit with an extra bounce in his step that could have either been from the post-coital bliss or from forgetting to walk more carefully in the lower gravity. Either way, certain parts of him jiggled in ways that Annabeth wasn't in the mood to watch.

What she did watch as she struggled out of the suit and pulled off her jumpsuit underneath, however, was his breakfast. His kitchen was barely worth the name, containing only a small stove, a mini-fridge, and a counter that had a few cupboards under it. However, this small nook in his apartment was still more than most people in Miranda had. Unlike Annabeth, who would have to make her way to the central mess hall soon, this guy actually got to make food for himself. He pulled out a small pitcher that appeared to contain some kind of juice and poured himself a glass – a real glass, not one of the air-tight sippy cup things everyone else got – then took out a pan, put it on the burner, and removed from the fridge...

"Is that an egg?" Annabeth asked. Despite her attempt to sound disinterested, her voice came out almost reverent.

Svensson grinned at her as he held it over the pan. "I have a second one, if you want it. You'll, uh, have to pay for it though."

Annabeth wanted to scoff at the idea, but suddenly she felt her stomach rumbling as she imagined that rich protein taste on her tongue. There were no chickens here, no livestock of any kind. This egg had been shipped here special. Math wasn't her strong suit, but she could come up with a very rough estimate of how much it was worth. The fuel, the planning, the engineering that it would have taken just to get that egg here in one piece, it had to cost thousands of United States dollars. In Rothschild company scrip, it would be worth more than she would earn during her entire five year stay in Miranda. She didn't want to think about all the depraved things this jackass would expect her to do in payment.

Still though, she hesitated to say no. It was an egg. An honest to God egg. Just one bite would be all she needed to clear her mind of that God-awful protein slop they served in the mess hall. Not even Leah Hartnup had access to something like this.

"I'll..." She forced the word to come out of her mouth. She was surprised at just how much effort it took. "...pass."

Svensson shrugged. Annabeth could tell from his shit-eating smirk that he knew just how close she had come to saying yes. She was sure she would pay for it later. At some point in the future she would have to service this ass again, and didn't like the thought that next time he might have something that could break her will.

The phone charging on Svensson's wall rang as Annabeth shimmied out of her jumpsuit. This thankfully occupied him as she bent over, naked from the waist down and pulled on her underwear. She didn't want him ogling her when he wasn't paying. He picked the phone up and asked what the hell the person on the other end wanted at this hour. Annabeth tried not to listen in on his conversation, since she didn't really care about or want to get involved in any of the petty drama among the management types.

"Well, so the fuck what?" he asked the phone. "Coms go down all the time. Why would I want to interrupt my breakfast for that?"

Someone mumbled something Annabeth couldn't hear, but whatever he said it must have struck a nerve. He looked over at Annabeth, then turned away from her. When next he spoke, it was in a voice slightly above a whisper.

"Look, I'm not alone... Yeah, that's right... So just give me a few minutes and I'll be right over."

Annabeth had gotten the legs of her environment suit back on by the time he hung up. "Okay sweetheart, time for you to get the hell out of here," he said. "Chop chop. I've got to get back to the business of keeping all your sorry asses alive." He actually snapped his fingers at her and pointed at the outer door. Annabeth resisted the urge to say something rude and obnoxious. Instead, she moved faster to get her environment suit back on. He dressed in his own jumpsuit, one that was decidedly newer and sleeker than her own, then stood tapping his foot impatiently at the inner door while she took a moment to inspect her suit for tears. He wouldn't need an environment suit to leave his apartment- the inner door led right into the administration wing- but if he had, Annabeth was sure it would be one of the slender, top of the line suits designed only a few years ago specifically to protect against all manner of hazards in any given emergency situation. Annabeth didn't have that luxury. When she had first arrived here three years ago, she'd been assigned an old and bulky repurposed Russian suit that had likely been made before she was even born. If something ripped at an inopportune moment, the tear wouldn't fill with emergency foam to keep the suit from depressurizing. Instead, she would have to run for the nearest shelter and hope someone would let her in before she asphyxiated or her blood started to boil.

When she was satisfied that she wouldn't die (at least not immediately) when she walked out the door, she finally went to the outer exit, pressed the button next to it, and walked into the airlock beyond. She looked back through the viewport in the door to see Svensson going through the inner door. That was odd. She'd never known one of the management types to leave her alone when she could still get back into the apartment. They had this paranoid idea that the "physical employees" of Miranda such as herself were just waiting for the perfect opportunity to rob them blind. In fact, given how much she disliked this dick, she had half a mind to do exactly that. Jeanette Weasel (she insisted that was her real name, although Annabeth doubted it) ran a healthy black market and Annabeth was sure she would pay some serious scrip for what Svensson had lying around his apartment.

But Annabeth really didn't want to lower herself to that level. She might rent her body out every night, but she had her standards. And she was too unnerved by Svensson's actions. She couldn't help but think something had to be wrong for him to leave that quickly. And something wrong in a place like Miranda meant there was something wrong for everybody.

She tried to push it from her mind. This was not her business. Her business was concluded until she got the next call from somebody with a little extra scrip to spend. Now it was time to simply go home and get some real sleep.

She pressed the button to depressurize the airlock and then, after putting her visor down against the sun rising on the horizon, stepped out onto the cold and desolate red desert that made up the entirety of the planet Mars.

3

When the Venture rover first made its amazing discovery seven years ago, the clamor on Earth had been unprecedented. For decades, the population at large had resisted the idea of sending humans to Mars. They had said it was too expensive. They had said there were better things to do with the taxpayers' money. They had said mounting missions outside their own planet was foolish and irresponsible when there were still so many problems that needed to be addressed at home. Of course, everybody had developed a completely different opinion when the siren song of Mars changed its tune from scientific growth and achievement to profit. Now that there was something valuable on Mars, people couldn't get to the red planet fast enough.

Out of the 156 people currently surviving on Mars, 155 of them had come here with dollar signs in their eyes. The upper management came to get rich, the science teams were looking for corporate sponsorship for their studies, and the lowliest workers just wanted steady employment. Leah Hartnup was the only person here for a reason other than money. Not to say that she wasn't getting paid like everyone else. Quite the contrary. While many of the people here were getting screwed by the system and barely surviving, she had a rather fat bank account that was getting fatter every moment she stayed here. She was here by choice, but only because her other option had been twenty years in prison.

Sometimes Leah wondered whether she had made the right choice. She had a lot more freedom here than she would have in jail. She had access to state of the art computers (or at least as state of the art as possible considering it took nearly five months to ship them here from Earth). She found herself working daily on interesting problems that kept her mind more or less occupied and, on the occasions where she got bored, the management turned a blind eye to her mischief as long as she didn't interfere with production and profits. And, of course, she got the bragging rights of being one of the first twenty-five people to set foot on another planet besides Earth and the moon.

Yet in its own way, Mars was still a prison. From where she stood now, she could look out a thick glass window and see a vista that had seemed spectacular and dreamlike when she had first come. Almost the entire world was a red desert. It was close yet not quite like something she might see on Earth, maybe in the American Southwest or the Australian Outback. Some areas around Miranda had been cleared of the random rocks that speckled the landscape, but only where they would interfere with the colony's operations. At certain times of the day the sky would lighten, but usually it was a rust color only a few shades lighter than the planet itself.

However, the subtle beauty of the planet had worn thin as the other aspects of the planet had made themselves more and more apparent. Whereas even the most desolate-looking place on Earth still had some form of animal or plant life desperately clinging to survival, Mars was completely barren. No form of life known to man other than perhaps a few highly adapted microbes could survive here without significant assistance. And for a desert it wasn't even warm. On certain rare occasions, the temperature could get as high as the fifties or sixties in Fahrenheit, but much more often it was bitterly cold, dropping into the negative hundreds in some places, depending on the season. It would be enough to flash freeze any human that dared walk outside unprotected. Before they could die of that, though, they would succumb to asphyxiation as they futilely tried to gain substance from an atmosphere that consisted mostly of carbon dioxide. The air pressure too, while far better than in open space or on the moon, was below what a human body could naturally stand.

It was an environment perfectly designed to kill anyone foolish enough to not follow the rules. In that way, it might as well have been another prison. It was far harsher than anything Leah had believed she was escaping.

Fortunately, if this was a prison, then Leah was in what would only be considered the cushy white-collar crime wing. Of the three Rothschild Syndicate colonies on Mars, Miranda was the biggest and most cramped, yet Leah didn't have to sleep in closet-like habitat modules like the largest portion of the population. Leah's expertise (and, on the rare occasions where she had nothing better to do with her time, her ability to use that expertise to find juicy ways to blackmail a handful of her superiors) afforded her the right to an apartment. It wasn't enough that she could have an apartment by herself – space in Miranda was tight enough that she still needed to share with a roommate – but at least she had been given the option to choose who she lived with. She'd chosen Annabeth Crick partly because she liked the girl's spirit and partly because she just loved the scandalized look on people's faces when they realized Leah roomed and was best friends with a working girl.

Annabeth hadn't slept in her bed last night, so it stood to reason that she'd had to pull another all-nighter. As she waited for her to come back, Leah busied herself getting ready for the day, putting on a fresh set of underclothes and jumpsuit before spending half an hour in the mirror putting on more makeup that anyone on Mars could possibly need. Like any luxury item here, makeup was ungodly expensive, but it was the only extra thing Leah allowed herself. She knew damned well all the possible psychological implications behind her makeup obsession, mostly because she'd seen the notes on her that she'd hacked from Dr. Bassinger's hard drive. The makeup was just another wall that she hid herself behind and so on and whatever. Maybe it was true and maybe it was bullshit. All she knew was that the people of Miranda had tendency to not mess with someone who intentionally made herself look vaguely like the Crow.

Every so often, Leah glanced out the window into the red morning light, expecting to see Annabeth lumbering across the landscape in her Russian environment suit. Leah would never say it to her face, but she worried about Annabeth deeply when she went out. Leah had tried to pull some strings to get Annabeth the privilege of travelling through the inner corridors for her assignations, or even at the very least to get her a suit that had been made within the last decade and didn't look like it should belong in a Cold War museum. But even if Leah was able to force some respect out of the management, she simply couldn't get it afforded to any of the working girls.

She continued to look out the small porthole of a window that provided her apartment's only view of the planet's surface, although she knew full well that wouldn't tell her much. Annabeth would be coming from the center of Miranda while Leah's window faced outward more toward the open pit of the mine. She wouldn't even know whether Annabeth was on her way until she heard the cycling of the airlock just down the hall from the apartment's only exit. She knew from her poking around in the official Rothschild files on Miranda's design that said airlock was only supposed to be used in the event of a catastrophic emergency. To the management, though, "catastrophic emergency" apparently included "we don't want 'those' kind of people walking around in the open of the management wing where we can be reminded of them." When Leah had first learned of this attitude shortly after she had gotten settled, she'd been horrified. The Rothschild Syndicate had gone to all the trouble and expense to send three extra women (women who of course weren't on any official list of Rothschild employees down on Earth) the 140 million miles to the Red Planet purely to "entertain" the management staff, but these women weren't even allowed the most basic safety of travelling in the corridors inside the building. It wasn't even like their presence here was a secret. Everyone, down to the lowliest worker mining out in the crater, knew Annabeth and the others were here and what they did, even using the working girls' services themselves on rare occasions. But the management's privacy was still more important to them.

Leah had asked Annabeth once why she'd never protested this. Rather than give Leah a straight answer, Annabeth had told her to put on the Russian suit. Although Leah had been trained in the proper way to put a suit on and check it for faults back before she had left Earth, she had not once had to wear one since arriving on Mars. There was an emergency suit in her apartment and the occasional emergency suit in various public places throughout Miranda but, as the computer and electronics expert of the colony, her job never required her to leave Miranda's safety. Not sure what Annabeth had been getting at, Leah had put the suit on quickly. The thing had been bulky, uncomfortable, and too big for her. Then Annabeth had told her to list off every single possible way in which the suit could fail and kill her out in the harsh Martian environment. Although Leah had been able to list off quite a few,

Annabeth had been able to list off many more, then pointed out that there were still a significant numbers she was probably missing.

Then Annabeth had asked Leah if she thought she would be able to sleep with one eye open and on the suit every time she went to service some upper-management type that she had pissed off by complaining about the conditions of her employment. Leah had gotten the point. She hadn't wanted to believe that anyone would do such a thing, but she got the point perfectly.

Leah knew full well she shouldn't be too concerned about Annabeth anymore. She'd gone on enough assignments in her year and a half (in Earth terms, not Martian) on the planet and she knew even better than Leah the proper safety measures to take. Still, Leah worried. Leah herself had been here just short of five years and she had seen first-hand what the harsh Martian landscape could do to anyone that made the slightest mistake. One person had died early on when a key seal on a hatch between habitat modules had failed. At least two people had died while mining. There was also the drunken murder that the Rothschild Syndicate had tried to keep hidden even from the people of Miranda. The person allegedly responsible had mysteriously "gone back to Earth" soon after, although Leah knew full well that there hadn't been a proper launch window back at the time. Outside of Miranda, there had been two other deaths, both of them in the Rochelle colony. Leah didn't know many details about those other than the fact that they were listed in all reports as "operator error." When there were only 156 people currently living on the planet, that many deaths was significant, although there would never be a graveyard to remind the residents. Current protocol was to cremate all the bodies at Rochelle, mostly because the effort to take them outside and dig a unique hole for the body was itself considered too dangerous and a waste of valuable Rothschild time and resources.

The more Leah reflected on all this, the more she wished she had taken the prison sentence instead.

Of course, then she would never have met Annabeth, and she wasn't sure if that would have been a fair trade. Leah had never had siblings, but she liked to imagine that any relationship she had with one would be exactly the same as her relationship to Annabeth. She thought of Annabeth as her little sister, even if technically she was Leah's senior by just over a year. In many ways, Annabeth was the less mature one, at least in Leah's view. She still had the idea that once her time on Mars was finished and she was able to go back to Earth she would find her one true love and settle down with two point five children, complete with a picket fence and a Golden Retriever in the back yard. Leah couldn't quite imagine any future for herself that rosy, nor did such a scenario even appeal to her. She had an on-again-off-again relationship here in Miranda with the resident biologist and she didn't want or expect anything more than the same when she returned. She also much preferred the idea of a trailer far enough from her native city of Cardiff that she could forget about the world, but close enough that she had no trouble getting Wi-Fi. In Leah's experience, that was a far more realistic expectation of what life was capable of giving a person even at the absolute best.

And yet Annabeth was smart, far smarter than any person on all of Mars gave her credit for. Yes, she was just one of the working girls, here for a variety of reasons that had absolutely nothing to do with her brains. Yes, she had been recruited for this position (through less than savory means, by Annabeth's account) from a spot microwaving frozen burgers in the American Midwest. But she had a college education and more street smarts than Leah had ever developed in her whole sheltered life. Just talking with her for a few minutes when Annabeth had first arrived was enough to make Leah realize this was a person she wanted in her life.

Besides, it wasn't like Leah had many other choices for friends around here. The miners and various maintenance workers treated Leah and her cushy position with disdain, while nearly everybody above her was pretty much an asshole. And it didn't help that she had to hide several major parts of her past thanks to the less than progressive background many of the others came from. If she hadn't become so close to Annabeth then Leah might very well have gone on to kill herself by now.

She looked out her tiny window again, knowing full well she wouldn't see any sign of her friend, but something about the scene outside bugged her and she couldn't understand why just yet.

Certainly it didn't look any worse than normal. Other than the occasional dust storm that would cause havoc with the mining site and bury portions of Miranda in red sand, there was rarely any change to the landscape. There wasn't even much weather to speak of, considering the lack of liquid water anywhere known on the surface of the planet. Without the dust, even the wind would have been negligible - winds could get up to nearly a hundred miles an hour at times, but if someone put their hand out in it the wind would have just feel like a gentle breeze, thanks to an atmosphere that was only one hundredth the density of that on Earth.

Of course, then that hand would probably freeze off, but still. It was an interesting factoid for Leah to know, even if it was completely useless to her.

No dust today, Leah suddenly realized. *None at all yet.* That was what looked so wrong about this scene. The mine should have been a flurry of activity by now, and even if she couldn't see inside the pit mine itself from this angle, she should have been able to see the cloud of dust rising up in the low gravity. But there was nothing. The miners, for whatever reason, weren't working yet.

"Somebody's going to be pissed about that," Leah muttered. She was flippant about it here by herself, but she knew that somewhere within the colony some management type would be having a fit right now. Maybe a vital piece of equipment had broken down. Maybe there was some problem with the miners. Whatever the answer, it still meant lost productivity. Leah was sure someone had a spreadsheet open right now as they calculated how many millions or even billions of dollars they were losing with every idle second.

Somewhere just outside her room, Leah heard a thump on the hard polymer outer walls, and she finally took a deep breath in relief. There were a few more thumps and scrapes as the outer hatch of the airlock first opened then closed, followed closely by the noise of motors filling the airlock with breathable air. Leah sat down in one of the room's two uncomfortable chairs and did her best to look like she hadn't just been pacing the room in worry. After another minute and some muffled cursing, Annabeth finally opened the door. She seemed to be having trouble with the latch on her helmet. Leah silently got up and helped her wrench the damned thing off before closing the door and allowing Annabeth to continue swearing in relative privacy.

"Fucking bullshit," Annabeth said. "I put in a requisition order nearly a month ago to have that latch fixed. Seriously, that can't be safe."

Leah nearly added her own complaints to Annabeth's rant, but after four years here she was tired of hearing it even from herself. Annabeth was too far down the ladder to have anybody pay any attention to her troubles, whether they posed a threat to her life or not. Leah had done everything she could to use her own influence to help Annabeth, but in this case she had found herself in the rare position of striking out completely. Even Leah's access into the maintenance database had been a bust this time. They were running low on the raw materials needed for the 3-D printers for her to make the necessary parts to fix Annabeth's suit herself. Until the next supply drop came in four months, the maintenance crew would be watching that supply closely, mostly because Leah herself had dipped into it one too many times herself and aroused suspicion.

Just five more months of this, Leah thought. *Five months and it's finally over*. Well, nine or ten months really when she added in the amount of time it would take to make it back to Earth, but she expected the five months cramped into the return craft to be a joyride compared to the Hell that was Miranda.

Annabeth stripped off her suit, making sure to give it yet another once over before hanging it next to her bunk, and then unzipped her jumpsuit underneath so she was in nothing but her underwear. That too she stripped off, not caring whether Leah saw her naked, before wrapping herself in a heavy blanket and making a slow Martian-gravity plop onto the bottom bunk. She grabbed her underwear and, after a moment's hesitation, gave it a hesitant sniff and wrinkled her nose.

"Ugh, smells like Svensson. You know, I really don't get it," Annabeth said. Leah smiled as her Southern American accent started to come out. Most of the time it vanished, unconsciously repressed from the constant barrage of accents and languages that flew around the colony on a daily basis. It only came out again when she was getting ready to go off on someone. "This guy is one of the top brass here. He can have anything he wants. Fuck, he doesn't even have to pay for me out of his own pocket- the Rothschild Syndicate picks up the tab for that. The bastard even had an egg for breakfast today. A fucking egg!"

Leah's mouth watered at that, but Annabeth didn't give her the chance to say so. "All of this, and you think he would take advantage of his free access to the chemical showers at any time. But no. If he ever goes anywhere near them, and I highly doubt he does, he evidently doesn't think screwing me is a special enough occasion. Not only do I have to sit there and smell him when he's behind me, but I'm forced to smell him when I get home too!"

Leah didn't bother to say anything. She instead walked over to the sealed laundry container she had brought home last night after Annabeth had left and opened it. She had heard this rant before. It didn't exactly annoy her, since she was perfectly happy to let Annabeth be the talker and her the listener, but Leah still knew nearly the entire thing by heart. Knowing she was going to hear it again this morning, Leah had taken care to be prepared this time.

She opened the container, pushed aside a few of her own underthings, and removed Annabeth's underwear. She'd scooped them all up from their place under the bunk and had them cleaned along with all her own underwear and jumpsuits. She tossed them at Annabeth, who squealed as she snatched them out of the air.

"Oh my God! You didn't!"

"I did," Leah said. Although she tried to maintain the dour expression she showed to most of the colony, Leah couldn't help but beam at the way Annabeth's face lit up.

"You didn't have to do that," Annabeth said. Nonetheless, she rubbed her cheek on the clean, crisp underwear as though it were a puppy. "That had to be expensive."

"Of course it wasn't. I just got into the cleaner's system and made it look like you'd already paid up for the next twenty or so sols." That wasn't true, although Annabeth didn't look for a second like she thought Leah was lying. While Leah's hacking skills were great, there was some stuff she couldn't do. The cleaning records weren't networked to any of the other systems and were effectively out of her reach, but most of the people throughout the three colonies wouldn't know enough about computers to call bullshit on the claim. In truth, Leah really had paid the expensive cleaning fees out of her own pocket. It had just seemed like something nice to do, and she wasn't a slave to the same pay system as people like Annabeth. Even if she'd been told that she would eventually return to Earth with huge amounts of money, the company scrip system the Syndicate used for its lowlier employees would likely send Annabeth home with barely anything to show for her time on the Red Planet. Leah, as a specialist that Rothschild wouldn't easily be able to replace when her time was up, was actually paid in real money and given what she was worth.

Annabeth finally realized that rubbing her underwear all over her face was less than normal and jumped up from the bed with a squeak of joy. She was so happy that she forgot about the low gravity and nearly hit her head on the ceiling. Once she was back on the floor, she tossed away the blanket and hurriedly slipped into the fresh underwear while Leah pulled out her bras and handed one to her. Annabeth took it but didn't even bother to hook it before she stopped and launched herself at Leah, giving her a hug that nearly knocked her over the one tiny table in their quarters.

Leah made a few requisite grouchy comments about Annabeth's enthusiasm even though she knew she wasn't fooling the woman. They both knew Annabeth was one of only two friends Leah had on this entire planet, and despite the intimate relationship Leah had with Dr. Martin Ruiz, Annabeth would be the only one that Leah would actively miss when she left.

Just four months, Leah thought as she hugged Annabeth back. *Four more months with my friend, four more months in this unforgiving tundra, and four more months in the employ of the Rothschild Syndicate*. She looked out the window again, out at center of the crater that should have been belching red dust to the sky already and the place where all this had started. She wouldn't miss most of it, but at the same time, she felt like she was about to be evicted from the only place that she had ever even remotely considered her home.

4

By the time the Venture Rover had landed by means of sky crane on the Martian landscape known as Tharsis, the public had simply not cared one way or other about the Red Planet anymore. At the beginning of the twenty-first century, there had been a resurgence of interest brought about by a series of probes and rovers - Curiosity, MAVEN, Mangalyaan. Each one had been successful, at least in terms of their actual missions. The general goal of most missions at that time had been testing the viability of life on Mars, past or future. The missions had all shown that there was promise. For a brief time, Mars had been on everybody's minds. Hollywood produced more movies about manned missions into space and grandiose plans were made for reality shows where contestants were trained to be among the first to set foot on a distant planet.

But that promise came in the slow manner of most scientific progress, and that had become a problem. Except for people of a certain mindset, watching multi-million dollar pieces of taxpayer-funded hardware slowly making their way over barren stretches of red desert to occasionally drill small holes in rocks didn't make for captivating video. And while scientists had urged patience, others had started to question why anyone was doing this. Politicians, in the effort to pander to a handful of constituents with less than a high school education, called for more and more cutbacks in space exploration programs. People watching their televisions and computers ignored the strings of numbers and data coming from sixty million miles away in favor of watching the latest reality TV show celebrity warn everyone that scientists didn't really know everything. Late night hosts searching for the lowest dangling fruit of comedy made jokes at the expense of engineers spending all their free time making sure a new type of wheel for the next rover worked.

That was usually the way things worked in space exploration. Interest grew and then faded before growing once again. Where the public was concerned, that was always the way when it came to space travel. And that was the way it would have continued to be if it weren't for the spectacular crash landing, broadcast around the world on a live internet feed, of the ADIS geological survey probe, resulting in the complete destruction of the most expensive unmanned Mars mission in history. Then, less than a month later, when Japan launched its own mission to put a permanent robotic weather station at the Martian South Pole, there was another accident. Someone along the chain of command forgot to follow the proper security protocols and a technician got caught underneath the rocket at liftoff. Although that had nothing to do with the planet itself, it still got the blame.

Mars, the public started to decide, was too dangerous to continue exploring, at least for now. Scientists resigned themselves to the knowledge that they would have to wait for public interest to come back around again, even if that was another thirty or forty years in the future. Whole programs were scrapped. Independent companies, not beholden to the public interest as much as they were to their investors, bought up what remained of the technology and missions that looked like they would never see the light of day.

All that remained was to finish up the missions that were already in progress while the rest of the people of Earth turned their interest back to wars, sports, which politician was screwing whom, and whatever the newest Hollywood starlet was wearing to the Academy Awards. In this way, the Venture Rover landed with only a tiny blurb on most news sites and the half-hearted jokes of the internet trolls commenting on them.

Venture, like so many rovers before it, had been created for the purpose of answering the single most enduring question about Mars: had the planet at any point in the past been capable of supporting life? To support life, any planet would need three things - a source of energy, water, and organic compounds. The energy on Mars, as on Earth, would have likely been the Sun, although it was possible that geothermic sources within the planet could have done the same. Water was trickier, especially considering the current Martian atmosphere was so thin that any water on the surface would either evaporate or, more likely on a planet which spent nearly all its time below the freezing point, sublimate directing from ice to gas. Yet past explorations had shown it highly likely that, at some point in millennia past, liquid water had been present on Mars. That only left the last component, organic compounds. On a planet that was only half the size of Earth but had roughly an equal amount of dry land, searching for something so small was a monumental task. Venture had been designed with this mission in mind.

After much debate about where to start searching, the researchers involved had decided to begin somewhere in Tharsis. Tharsis was a plateau in the planet's western hemisphere that was home to some of the most impressive known landmarks in the entire solar system. In its east was Valles Marineris, an immense canyon roughly the length of the United States. The rest was volcanic in nature and was home to a number of giant volcanoes including Olympus Mons, the single largest volcano humans had yet discovered.

The idea had been that, if there was ever any place where organic molecules might come about and thrive on such a desolate planet, it would be near the Tharsis volcanoes. So that was where the rover had touched down, approximately 150 kilometers north of the long-dormant volcano Pavonis Mons, and began its search.

Over the next eleven months, the Venture rover slowly crawled north, powered by solar cells, a small nuclear engine, and supported by a remote crew of just under a hundred people on Earth. The support crew had originally been intended to be much larger, but those jobs had been yet another casualty of cutbacks across the board to all space programs. Those same cutbacks continued. As the months passed, the Venture support crew dwindled to eighty, then sixty, and finally forty. While Venture never found the organic traces it was searching for, it continued to gather and send incredible amounts of data, information that could have been valuable to anyone and everyone studying Mars if only there were enough people to analyze it all and make sense of it. The backlog of data increased until NASA was forced to simply dump the raw info on a huge website and hope that the dwindling numbers of citizen scientists could make something of it.

Nine months and twenty-six Earth days after landing, the Venture rover found itself at the outer ejecta of Poynting Crater, approximately 110 kilometers from Venture's initial landing site. The earliest mission parameters had stated that this was the point where Venture would turn east and head in the general direction of Ascraeus Mons, where, if Venture still failed to get its holy grail of organic molecules, it would at least be able to study the rock formations of an otherworldly volcano. This was when the thirty six remaining people looking after the Venture mission had to stop and have a discussion.

It had become obvious to all of them that the days of the mission were numbered. Every single one of them could argue until they were blue in the face that it was a colossal waste to spend almost a billion dollars to send a state of the art robot rover to Mars and then abandon it, especially when it was still in perfectly good condition and sending back data. The politicians and the American taxpayers, though, obviously didn't see it that way. All they saw were overpaid eggheads sitting all day around a bunch of screens staring at red rocks. Talks were going on at that point about cutting staff yet again. The Venture scientists and engineers saw the way that things would go in the future. They knew Venture would never make it to even the outer edges of Ascraeus Mons. The rover would be abandoned halfway there and get chalked up in the history of the space program as another embarrassing failure.

After many heated arguments, the Venture crew eventually turned the rover away from Ascraeus Mons and toward Poynting Crater. It was a far less interesting target than the volcano, especially since there didn't seem to be much about Poynting that differentiated it from hundreds of other craters that pocked the surface of the Red Planet. It was simply the nearest landmark the Venture team believed they could reach before they expected to be shut down. That sort of deviation from mission parameters would have been unheard of at one point in time, but the truth everyone knew by then was nobody was paying attention to them anyway. They could have used the rover to draw a giant middle finger in the dust pointing back at Earth and no one would have noticed. The Poynting Crater plan, at least, would give them some sort of data that people might be able to take a closer look at when the human race collectively pulled its head out of its ass (a statement that was recorded for posterity but that none of the people involved would admit to saying later) and realized Mars was more than just a tiny red dot in the sky that barely affected their lives.

And so that was the direction Venture went. It was a single decision that would change the entire course of human history.

Halfway through the tenth month of the mission, Venture crested the rim of the crater and began poking around inside Poynting. Nobody in the outside world noticed, as this was right around the time of the World Cup and the match between Portugal and Austria was being hotly debated and bet upon.

As the tenth month became the eleventh, the Venture team was down to twenty-nine people. Once inside the crater, the rover had begun to examine several rocks almost haphazardly with the team no longer putting much rhyme or reason into what they had the rover examine and what it ignored. Despite this, however, they started to see something they had not seen anywhere else on Mars. Although the traces were small, chemical analysis of the dust in Poynting Crater had found unique carbon chains. This, the team believed, had the potential to lead them to exactly what they had been hoping for in the beginning. All they needed was a chain that included not only carbon but hydrogen. Meteorites believed to be from Mars had shown the presence of such chains in the past, but that hadn't been enough to prove that the organic compounds had originated from Mars. It could have just been contamination from when they had crashed to Earth. But finding those chains here would have proven all those theories and once and for all shown that it was possible for life to have at one point been on Mars.

They released these findings, but still no one else paid attention. Instead, the biggest trending topic on social media that week was a scandal involving the British Prime minister, a French gymnast, their hotel room in the Riviera, and a goat.

At eleven months, eight days, and fourteen hours into the Venture mission, with one more member of the team having just tendered her resignation two hours earlier, Venture snapped a picture. It took seven minutes for the signal to reach Earth, and another four for anyone from the overworked and punchy team to look at it. The first person didn't even see anything out of the ordinary. It was the second, a young man named Percy Lloyd who would become an international star in his own right in just a matter of days, who looked at the picture on his screen, stared at it for several minutes, and then finally said out loud, "What is that?"

"That" was a small light spot half-buried in the dirt. The odd color didn't necessarily mean anything. Things like that had been spotted before. It could have been gypsum, which so far hadn't been present in abundance in this region and, to a number of scientists, would have been a satisfying enough discovery. It could have been some piece of the Rover that had been broken or scoured off, which would have been worrying but not unprecedented. One theory, at once implausible and exciting, was that it was ice from just below the surface that had been revealed by the winds and captured on camera before it sublimated.

Whatever it was, it was deemed interesting enough for Venture to get closer and investigate. It continued to send back footage all the while. The light bright spot didn't vanish, telling them it couldn't be ice. Once Venture was close enough, it performed its typical chemical analysis, a process that took several minutes.

The instant the results appeared on the monitors in the Venture mission headquarters, every single person stopped and stared. Not one word was said until someone got on a phone to tell the higher ups that something had been discovered. Something big.

Venture had confirmed that the tiny stone it had found was carbon. But it didn't have the hydrogen they had been looking for that made it an organic molecule. Instead, it was a metastable allotrope of the element arranged in a face-centered cubic crystal structure. Initially, it was believed that this had to be some kind of mistake with the sensors, but close inspection of the images Venture continued sending back to Earth showed more stones. Analysis of every one it found gave the same results.

For the two days before the findings were announced, scientists stayed behind closed doors debating how this all could possibly be. Geologists asserted that, given the volcanic nature of the area, the formation of what they had found was certainly a possibility while others argued that the stones might not be Martian in origin at all. They could have been from whatever it was that had crashed into the planet and created Poynting Crater to begin with. It was a debate that would rage for years, and up until the moment that

Leah and Annabeth shared their awkward semi-naked hug over the idea of clean underwear, it was still an argument that remained unsettled.

Before the press conference that finally announced Venture's discovery, the world was perfectly prepared to continue ignoring anything and everything having to do with the Red Planet. After all, there were celebrities to ogle, petty wars to fight over long forgotten feuds, and political maneuverings to be made. Very few people throughout the world bothered to watch the initial press conference live. The number of hits it would receive afterward, however, would number in the billions as people watched and rewatched the news: diamonds had been discovered on Mars.

Finally, the world was paying attention to the Red Planet.

5

Considering there were over 150 people living on Mars, ostensibly all there for the purpose of mining diamonds for the Rothschild Syndicate and sending them back to Earth, Dip always marveled that there were so few miners. At no time had there ever been more than fourteen and at this moment, while they were all waiting around in their full suits waiting for permission to head out the airlock for work, there were only eight. Anil Khan, one of only two miners other than Dip who came from India, was currently in the infirmary still recovering from injuries he'd sustained when a piece of equipment had fallen on his foot, nearly crushing it, eight sols ago. In all likelihood, he would be headed back to Earth with the next launch off world in five months.

While the loss of any worker made the job more difficult for everyone around them, it wasn't quite as difficult as it would have been if this were a typical Earth mine. Most of the difficult and dangerous work here was done by robotic rovers similar, yet smaller, to the Venture rover that made the discovery in the first place. The miners were there to provide just enough maintenance to get the rovers back to the airlocks in the event of a problem and, more often than not, do random grunt work that wasn't worth the Rothschild Syndicate sending yet another multi-million Euro robot to do.

All that machinery was currently in a shed just outside the airlock to keep it safe from the elements while the men waited around in here. Dip knew something had to be wrong if they hadn't gotten the all-clear over their coms to go out yet, but he couldn't guess at what. A delay of any kind was not common. Rothschild didn't allow it, and anyone who got in the way of their perfectly oiled operation was removed immediately. Like Anil. Although no one would say so aloud, it was an open secret that he wouldn't be getting any of the money that was owed to him – not even what little was left after the Syndicate had bled him dry with the expenses, fees, and hidden charges that came with living in the

Miranda colony. By breaking his foot and being forced back to Earth, he was technically breaking his contract, so instead of the humongous payday that had been promised to each and every miner on this crew, he would end up actually owing the Rothschild Syndicate enough money that he probably wouldn't be able to pay it all back in his lifetime. After over two years here, that was a harsh fate to face. No other person on this crew would trade places, even if they could, to spare him.

Except, Dip realized, that wasn't entirely true. At this point, he himself might have been willing to switch places with Anil if it were at all possible, especially given what little he had heard Sendhil say about Mallika before the v-mail had gone dark. Dip didn't have a wife and children like Anil did, despite his parents continued insistence that he allow them to arrange a marriage for him. The idea of a family depending on him wasn't appealing, especially if he would have kept worrying about them while he was off having his grand interplanetary adventure. Or at least that had been the idea. Being on an entirely different planet should have provided enough distance to keep others from interfering with his life. The only person that would have made him change his mind about that, of course, was exactly the one who was now sick.

He tried to tell himself that it was probably nothing. Mallika was pregnant with her first child, and Sendhil was probably exaggerating what was wrong with her. The next time he received a v-mail it would say that Mallika had just been suffering from morning sickness, nothing more, and Sendhil was just getting the expectant parent jitters.

But what if something is wrong? Dip thought. *What if something happens to her and I'm not there?* It was an old worry that went to the earliest days of their childhood. Mallika was the older sibling but she had always been the sweet, shy one that wouldn't make waves. Dip had been the hothead, a temperament he'd mostly managed to shed with age, but in his mind he was still the only one who could make sure Mallika got all he believed she deserved in life.

No, he decided. He didn't need to be there with her. She had chosen the life she'd wanted and he'd chosen his. Still, Sendhil's few words about her had stuck with him.

She was vomiting all night… feverish… take her to the doctor if it doesn't stop soon…

Dip would have lit a lamp of ghee to Dhanvantari, if there had been any ghee on Mars, as a way to ask for her health. Instead, he'd had to settle with a simple prayer before getting to the mess hall and then into his suit. He'd thought the work would take his mind off everything. Instead, he was stuck here waiting, still thinking about it, and having to listen to all the others as they complained.

As usual Roy Osbourne, one of the two Americans on the mining team, was talking the loudest and with an abundance of curse words so creative that Dip wasn't sure how to translate them into his native language of Marathi. Even if Dip turned off his radio, he was sure he would have still heard Roy. Jay Davis, the other American, occasionally responded to Roy, usually in a half-hearted attempt to get him to calm down. The two of them stood off to the side, some distance away from the others. Jay never seemed to have any problem with anyone else on the team, considering he was soft spoken and quick to lend an ear to anyone that needed it. Roy on the other hand treated everyone else here like garbage. He'd been here from near the beginning of the colony and seemed to think that made him superior, despite the fact that not a single other person on the team respected him.

On a long bench near the airlock usually reserved for people putting on and taking off their suits, three of the men sat, their helmets taken off fifteen minutes ago when it had become apparent that they wouldn't be going out onto the surface any time soon. If someone in management had come along and found anyone else here with their helmets off, even despite the wait so far, there would have been some kind of punishment but two of the three tended to get some leeway. William York, the oldest man on the mining crew at thirty-six, was a dark-skinned Brit while Ravi Gavankar was from Bombay. The two were unique among the miners in that they had been picked out specially, rather than chosen through the lottery system used to select and hire the rest of the miners, because they were willing to act not only has grunt workers but also as spiritual leaders. While a long list of complaints could be leveled at the Rothschild Syndicate regarding how they had set up the system on the three colonies of Mars, one of the few things Dip acknowledged that they had done right was to make sure the people's religious needs would be met. William acted as a Christian pastor for those who worshipped that way, while Ravi was a pujari for anyone, like Dip, that counted themselves Hindu. The Syndicate likely would have included a Muslim holy man as well if there were more than just the one - Parviz Hosseini, the third man on the bench. Long before the Martian diamonds had been discovered, back in the beginning of the twenty-first century when Mars had been experiencing one of its resurgences in popularity, a group of imams in the United Arab Emirates had issued a fatwa declaring it against Islam for Muslims to go to Mars. It had been their thought that any trip to Mars would likely be one-way and therefore tantamount to suicide. Some Muslims had taken that to heart while Parviz had disagreed. Just because he had gone against a fatwa didn't diminish his beliefs, though, and the three of them could often be seen together in friendly but intense discussions about religion.

The remaining two stood next to Dip yet kept their distance from Roy. Dev Jaffrey was of Indian descent, even if he had never lived there, while Arne Bergland was a native of Sweden. While he didn't have the official title, Dev acted as the foreman of the crew. Dip had little problem with Dev and even had some respect for the man. He was fair and knew his way around the mining equipment better than anyone, even if he was a little short on patience. That lack of patience had bothered Dip at first, yet Dev had gotten much better about it after Arne had started.

The crew as a whole used a mess of languages among themselves but the two most commonly used ones were English and French. Arne, unfortunately, hadn't been able to speak a word of either at first, only being able to speak his native Swedish and a little German. Dev, thankfully, had also known a little German and he had taken Arne under his wing. They had quickly learned that their limited German wasn't the only thing they'd had in common, though, and although they'd tried to hide it from the rest of the crew at first, they had become lovers. Dip personally was happy they had each other, as it made them both happier and easier to work with. The rest of the group had shown a mixed reaction across the board, ranging from Jay and Parviz's easy acceptance to Roy's completely unhidden disgust.

"Hey, you," Roy said, apparently interrupting himself in mid-rant to Jay and directing his new words to Dev. As far as Dip could tell, Dev didn't have a proper name in Roy's tiny mind and hadn't since the moment Dev and Arne's relationship had become obvious. Not that he typically called anyone else on the crew by their names on a regular basis except for Jay. Whenever Roy thought he was alone or was pretended he thought he was alone (all the while completely intending for the others to overhear him while feigning his innocence), he tended to let loose with a string of racial slurs for every single person on the crew. Jay never spoke up about this but at least had the decency to look mortified by Roy's words.

Dev gave Roy nothing more than a cursory glance before turning back to Arne and continuing their own conversation in an odd mix of German and French.

"Hey, don't you fucking ignore me," Roy said. "Why the hell are we still sitting here, huh? We don't actually get paid for any moments we're inside. Every moment you don't let me out to do my work you're stealing from me."

Dip almost corrected him, but he didn't see the point in trying anymore. That wasn't true at all. As soon as they'd put their cards in the punch clock after suiting up they were officially getting paid. Everyone knew that, including Roy, but he didn't care. He was just looking for another reason to give Dev a hard time. Dev, for his part, didn't rise to the bait. He only rolled his eyes and kept talking with Arne.

"Hey, I'm fucking talking to you," Roy said. "And when I talk you better answer me."

Dip really wished he could say this was an uncommon outburst for Roy, except it wasn't. Multiple people on the crew had complained about him in the past, but the management had yet to do much more than give him a stern talking to which was promptly ignored. It had angered Dip early on. In an environment as harsh and unforgiving as the one they worked in every day, he would have expected the Syndicate to want less disharmony. The

Rothschild Syndicate didn't care, though, as long as the diamonds kept coming. The official rules against harassment were nebulous and didn't even appear to be written down anywhere that anyone could see. That state of affairs would never have been allowed in most of their home countries back on Earth, but they were millions of miles from any recognized nation or its laws.

"I do not know, Roy, and if you continue this I will report you," Dev said.

Roy came away from the wall where he'd been leaning and took several steps toward Dev. Dip was sure the movements were supposed to be menacing, but even after all this time on Mars, Roy had still not managed the trick of such a thing when every step had an extra spring.

"I'm not scared of you, faggot," Roy said.

Dip's English might have been basic but he had heard the word enough from Roy to understand the deep insult in it. He knew how Dev would react. While no one had much faith that management would do anything effective to punish Roy, Dev would still report the incident and the slur by the book. He might be angry and cursing the entire time he was doing it, but that was simply the way he worked. He had said before, where Dip could hear, that you had to have faith in the system even when it didn't work because eventually it would and all would be balanced.

Dip decided that wouldn't be good enough for today. Even as he stepped between Roy and Dev, he realized that, on any other day where he wasn't worried for the health of one of the few people he cared about, he would never do this. But the v-mail from Sendhil had gotten him into the wrong mood, a mood Mallika would never approve of. But Mallika and her calming presence weren't here. Besides, Dip was thoroughly tired of this man.

"Back away, Roy," Dip said. He spoke in French, since he was more certain of the finer points of that language than he was with English. He knew Roy understood him, but he refused to answer in anything but English.

"Fuck off, dot-head," Roy said. "This has nothing to do with you and everything to do with finally showing this faggot who—"

Dip hit him. Immediately, he regretted it. Not because he cared one way or other what happened to Roy, but because he knew the

Rothschild Syndicate would have a fit if he harmed the precious suit Roy was currently in.

It wasn't even that strong of a hit. The padding and awkwardness of both their suits kept Dip from giving him much more than a tap, yet Roy hadn't expected it and it was enough to send him stumbling back to the bench. William and Parviz managed to get out of his way in time but he hit Ravi butt first, sending them both sprawling backward over the bench. For several seconds, Roy was nothing more than a cloud of curse words, half of which Dip didn't even understand, and a hurricane of flailing limbs that did little to put him back into an upright position. By the time he extricated himself from Ravi, his white cheeks had flushed to a furious red, and the look on his face when he stood up was a curious mixture of rage and deep confusion that such a thing could have possibly happened to him.

"You piece of shit!" Roy did his best to jump over the bench and come at Dip, a movement that should have been fairly easy but was doomed to failure thanks the mad, child-like kicking he did in the air. His boot caught on the bench and he went sprawling on the floor again, this time face first. Dip backed away but kept his fists up just in case this pathetic excuse for a man somehow managed to find enough dignity to stand again.

Before anything more could happen, Arne was in front of Dip, his hand on Dip's chest to keep him from going in for another punch. Jay did the same with Roy, holding him by the shoulders and, Dip noticed, keeping him on his knees for the moment so Roy couldn't stand. Dev stood between both of them and detached his helmet, probably the better to let both of them hear him screaming at them.

"Stop it or you're both on the next transport back to Earth!" Dev said in English. "You know the rules. If I report this, you're gone and the next person on Rothschild's waiting list takes your place."

"You can't be serious," Roy said. "I didn't do anything wrong. That fucker is the one that hit me! You're the faggot in charge here, so do your Goddamned job and send him home!"

"Oh my God, Roy," Jay said quietly over the coms. "Just be quiet before you truly put yourself in trouble."

"Me?" Roy said. "I'm the one who was wronged here."

Arne asked something in German and Dev answered him before Arne shrugged and responded.

"What?" Roy asked. "What did he say?"

Dev paused before he answered. It was clear to Dev that he was trying desperately not to smile. "He said that all he saw was you punching first. After that he lost track."

"You... you can't be fucking serious," Roy said. He finally pushed Jay's hands away and got to his feet, then turned around to look at every other person around him. "You people can't let him get away with that."

Ravi, still sitting on the floor and fiddling with his suit to make sure it wasn't damaged, gave Dip a quick glare of disapproval. That, however, didn't keep him from saying. "That is what I saw, too."

Parviz, unlike Dev, didn't try to hide the giant grin on his face as he nodded. "Don't look at me, Roy. I'm just a... what is it you called me last week? Raghead? Camel monkey? No, wait. That was the week before. Last week I was just a terrorist."

William was the only one who seemed conflicted about what to say. Dip suspected he had a serious problem with the idea of, as he always called it, "bearing false witness." In the end, however, all he did was throw his hands up in the air and turn his head aside as if to say he had nothing to do with this. Dip suspected he might have even taken Roy's side if Roy didn't always make the same horrible joke about William's skin color coming from traveling in space without his sun block.

Roy turned to Jay. "You. Jay. I know you'll back me up. People like us have to stick together, right?"

Jay looked absolutely horrified. Dip didn't know a lot about him. He knew Jay was from some town in Indiana and had a wife back home, possibly named Emily if Dip was remembering correctly. Beyond that, Jay had never made much of an impression on Dip. He would have had a problem with anyone who willingly made friends with a person like Roy, except he never saw Jay actually do anything to encourage a friendship. It was more like Roy was the one who wanted Jay's companionship purely by virtue of them being the only two white people on the mining crew and Jay just went along with it because he was afraid to make waves.

"Roy, I don't think it's a good idea to challenge this," Jay said. If he spoke any quieter, Dip would have wondered if something had gone wrong with his com.

Roy looked at everyone around him one more time, the expression of incredulity on his face slowly turning to rage. He looked like he was about to say something, possibly something that would really put his foot in his mouth and force it to permanently stay there, when they finally heard a voice from the intercom on the wall next to them.

"Morning mining schedule canceled," the voice said. It was so tinny that Dip couldn't even be sure who was speaking, although the accent sounded vaguely German. That alone was highly bizarre. Usually Mikhail Svensson and his Swedish accent were the ones giving the crew orders.

Dev went over to the panel and pushed a button to talk. "I just want to confirm. You want us to get out of our suits and… do what exactly?"

There was a long pause before there was any answer. "Morning mining schedule cancelled," the voice said again, although this time it sounded uncertain and questioning. There were some noises on the other end as though the person was shuffling around, and then this time a voice came on with a clear American accent.

"You can get out of your suits and punch out. Don't worry, I'll make sure you get paid for the time you've been waiting. You're free until after 1330 hours. We expect everything to be back to normal by then. We'll tell you all if the situation is otherwise, so be ready to go back to your normal work schedule at that point."

The intercom went silent. Dev tried to push the button again to ask further questions but no one on the other end answered.

"We're actually getting half a day off," Parviz said. "It's our lucky day." Ravi chuckled. Everyone else started taking off their suits in silence. Most of them were probably unnerved by the incident only minutes before, and although Dip knew he should be worried that someone would snitch on him, he was more concerned with the odd circumstances of their unexpected break. Never in the time that he'd been here had anyone in management given the mining crew a day off, even a partial one, if something wasn't wrong. Why would they, when every single tiny Martian diamond they found was worth billions of Euros back on Earth?

Even more disturbing to him, though, was something others didn't seem to have realized. None of them had given any consideration to the voice they'd just heard. That was probably because the mining crew so rarely heard it, but Dip recognized it as belonging to Tasha Westin. Westin was the director of all three Martian colonies, the highest up in the chain of command without going back to Earth and the three Rothschild siblings themselves. She never graced the mining crew with her presence because, even if the diamonds they found were their entire reason for being here in the first place, she had much more important things to worry about on a daily basis. Namely, she was the one who ensured they had air, that the interiors never dropped to the bone-chilling deep freeze of outside, that energy kept flowing from Rochelle, that food kept growing in the Kurtis colony. In short, her number one purpose, despite all the complaints anyone and everyone could lay on her, was to ensure that every living thing on Mars continued to live.

So what, Dip wondered, did that mean that she was suddenly poking her head out where others could hear her? He didn't know, and he wasn't sure he even wanted to. With any luck, everything would be back to normal this afternoon.

In the meantime, all Dip wanted to do was get out of this suit and back to his tiny room in the habitats. Hopefully there would be another v-mail from Sendhil, this time with more information about Mallika, and just as importantly, no abrupt end this time.

6

Tasha Westin, the woman that many considered to be the most powerful and important person on all of Mars, had severe trouble when it came to not biting her nails. It had been a nervous habit of hers ever since she was a kid, but it was the only nervous thing anybody ever saw from her, she made sure of that. Usually she kept herself from doing it around others, which was good considering it would have been a pretty big tell in situations where she needed to look like she was the one person in the room with the most control. Like now.

The urge to stick the end of her right pinkie finger in her mouth and go to town on an uneven nail stayed with her as she sat back down at the table. Everyone important was here now even if she hadn't started the meeting yet. It had been delayed at first as they had waited for Svensson to get his ass dressed and down to the meeting room. Svensson had taken his normal seat to Westin's right, as though he thought that meant something terribly important. Westin had promptly wrinkled her nose and backed away from the stench of sweat and sex still wafting off his body. She would have delayed the meeting long enough for everyone to take a chemical shower if all signs hadn't pointed to something bad brewing.

The meeting room where they currently sat was the biggest room out of all three of the Rothschild colonies on Mars, a fact that had always struck Westin as yet another example of the Syndicate's bizarre and messed-up priorities when it came to this entire planet. Most of the people were forced to live in MDRS habitat modules, a fancy way to say "cramped two-story cylinders full of closets." People that the Syndicate considered slightly more important got apartments that could at least be considered full rooms, even if they did have to share them. The ones who were highest up the chain (basically every person currently in this room or joining in the meeting through telepresence monitors) had the privilege of living in apartments large enough to be divided into actual rooms, the Martian equivalent of a palatial estate. Yet all of them were dwarfed by this room, which housed nothing more than a massive oak table (oak, for Christ's sakes!) and surrounded by enough chairs to seat about twenty. Westin had been the director of the Martian colonies for their entire existence, yet at no time had she ever had any need for all the chairs at once.

Instead, the entire senior ruling council of the Rothschild colonies took up only seven chairs and two screens. The fact that there were so many empty seats made Svensson's insistence on sitting right next to her all the more annoying. Westin liked to think that she was good at her job. She didn't hesitate to make the hard decisions when she had to, yet could act as the friendly public face of the Syndicate's presence whenever a softer touch was required. Despite her ability to act personable, though, she'd always had a problem when it came to being in close proximity to others. The psychologist who had vetted her for the job had stopped short of calling it "social anxiety." Westin thought of it as an extreme introversion, and it was that need to often be alone and far from others that allowed her to think and keep this place running. Svensson apparently didn't get that. He didn't get a lot of anything really. Westin thought of him as a blunt tool, a man whose management style lacked precision. If it had been her choice, he wouldn't be here and in charge of the commercial operations, but she had never had a say and the Rothschild siblings had never seen fit to give her a reason why they would send him and not someone else.

The rest of the senior staff, thankfully, was better at taking hints and sat at more spaced out places around the table. The closest, sitting several chairs down on Westin's left, was Dr. Mario Pereira. He tended to be surly and quiet, two traits that Westin doubted he would show in such abundance on Earth. In the Rothschild Syndicate's initial worldwide search for the best of the best to send to Mars (or, in the case of the lowlier workers, the most desperate), few positions had been more fiercely fought over than Pereira's. As the Chief Science Advisor, he oversaw the work of every other scientist throughout the three colonies, and the job had been seen among the scientific community as the single greatest position ever in the history of science. Once Pereira had arrived here, however, he was greeted with the unfortunate truth that any and all scientists were basically here as window dressing. The Rothschild Syndicate didn't care one way or the other about scientific advancement unless it resulted in more precious gems. Any other scientific presence on the colony was ignored, underequipped, and underfunded.

There were two other people on Pereira's side of the table, both near the far end. Takibana Ishikawa was the colony's head of security, while Martin Freelis was the water plant manager. The only person sharing Svensson's side of the table was Hans Metzger, Deputy Director and Westin's second-in-command here in the Miranda colony. Westin couldn't help but think of him as little more than a bean counter, but she intended that affectionately. As long as he didn't have to go outside his comfort zone as far as duties, he was second to none and Westin knew she could count on him. It was only when he had to deviate from his normal routine in any way, and that included his rather unsuccessful attempt at calling the miners away from the airlock minutes earlier, that he became flustered and tended not to know what to do. That was fine by Westin, however. She would prefer not to give any of the truly important duties of running the colony to anyone other than herself anyway. Too many people depended on her to ever think about taking anything like a break.

Darlene Anguitine sat at the other end of the table, the only person sitting completely straight with her hands folded neatly in front of her. That was a habit, Westin knew, that she had picked up during her stint as a talking head on one of the major US news channels, although Westin could never remember which. Her current job wasn't much different, considering she was Head of Martian Media Relations and any carefully vetted and edited video footage that left the Red Planet for Earth usually had her disturbingly plastic face and stiff smile bookending it. She was one of the few people on the planet that Westin couldn't technically say she was in charge of. She was more like a separate force that, just like Westin, answered directly to the Syndicate. Westin couldn't stand her, although it was tough to say why. Anguitine was never anything short of polite, never stepped on any toes, never pushed or prodded or asked for anything more than she absolutely needed to properly do her job. That, Westin thought, was part of what made her so creepy. She had no friends and no enemies, never even voiced an opinion as far as Westin ever heard. Sometimes Westin wondered if it might be a good idea to check Anguitine's medical records and be sure she was human, not some experimental android, but she resisted that urge. This was real life, after all, not science fiction.

There were cameras in front of each person at the table sending their images to the Kurtis and Rochelle colonies, and in turn, two of the telepresence monitors on the walls were beaming back live video of the two other Deputy Directors. Anna Gromov was in charge of Rochelle while Peter Renner oversaw the Kurtis colony. While the three colonies were technically separate and autonomous from each other, both of them still answered to Westin. She was grateful that both of them had proven far more capable in their positions than Metzger, since there was between fourteen and thirty kilometers separating each of the colonies and there would be little Westin could immediately do should something go catastrophically wrong at either of them.

Westin's job would have been much easier if there was only one large colony rather than the three smaller ones. Miranda, as the primary production base, had no choice but to be located in Poynting Crater with the diamonds. Rochelle, the largest source of energy for all three colonies, produced a large portion of that energy from geothermal sources which they had only been able to locate closer to the dormant volcanoes. Kurtis, the primary source of manufacturing and food production, was situated roughly between them to break up the distance that would need to be travelled over the harsh landscape. The Rothschild Syndicate often talked about sending the colonies the equipment needed to create tunnels between the three colonies, but like any other priorities beyond immediate diamond production, they tended to forget about those kinds of things.

"Okay," Westin said. The urge to bite her nails, even here right in front of all the most important people on Mars, was immense. There had been plenty of meetings between all of them in the past, even the occasional secret meeting in the dead of night. Those in particular were meetings she would never forget no matter how much she wanted, and she knew she would have to live with the knowledge of what they had done in the name of keeping the colonies safe and secure. So this meeting should have been nothing. All she had to report at the moment were rumors and educated guesses. It should have been easy.

Westin was absolutely terrified, and she didn't want the words to come out of her mouth. That would make them real.

"I do hope this is important," Svensson said. "I will not be the one to take the blame for the shutdown in mining operations. Do you know how much money the Syndicate is losing right now?"

"I know exactly how much, Mikhail," Westin said. "Don't go acting like you know better than I do."

She had hoped he would take the hint and shut up. He answered quietly, more to himself than anyone else. "Hundreds of millions."

He was figuring far too low. Westin knew the true answer was in the billions. While she was not a gemologist, she had been overseeing the colonies long enough to know the full value of the Mars diamonds. Mars diamonds contained unique microscopic carbon flaws that gave them a muddy pink or red color, even the ones that were found further beneath the surface where the dust wasn't actually red. For any diamond on Earth, those carbon flaws would have made them worth less than clear flawless diamonds. However, the nature of their origin made the "Martian Reds" the most sought after gemstones on Earth. The hottest up and coming starlets wanted to wear them on the red carpet at awards shows and tech billionaires like to have them around to show off exactly how offensively rich they were. Anyone holding a Martian Red was temporarily worth enough money to feed the population of entire countries for years.

And that wasn't the only cost to consider when it came to shutting down operations. Simply by sitting around this table and breathing, the seven people in this room were costing the Syndicate a fortune back on Earth. The air was such a valuable commodity that the Syndicate had quietly slipped a clause into the contracts of most of the workers on the planet that a small breathing fee would be taken out of their total pay when they returned to Earth. Beyond the expenses of just keeping air flowing and recycling through the colonies, there were also all the other materials, ranging from essentials like the environment suits and the habitats everyone lived in to the ridiculously inane like the table. Simply transporting everything here required engineering feats that had never before been attempted by humanity, and all of that cost the Syndicate money.

All of these were facts that the Rothschild Syndicate made sure Westin was aware of on a regular basis. So she knew much better than anyone else here exactly how much this temporary shutdown was costing.

Given what little Westin knew about what was happening on Earth, she quite frankly didn't give a rat's ass about lost revenue right now.

"This is about the launch, isn't it?" Freelis asked. "Did something go wrong?"

"To the best of my knowledge, the launch went fine," Westin said. She understood why some of them would be concerned, since up until late yesterday afternoon it had been her main concern as well. While the colonies were theoretically at a point where they could remain self-sufficient for up to three years at a time, there were always small mishaps that, when not taken care of immediately, would eventually put the lives of every person on the planet at risk if they weren't dealt with. These kinds of events could be small but daily, like micrometeors putting tiny holes in the habitats that required regular maintenance, or they could be catastrophic, like the nuclear coolant breach at Rochelle that Westin had needed to quietly cover up just over a year ago. All these things put a drain on their supplies far faster than the Syndicate liked to admit, and the regular supply capsules from Earth were eagerly awaited, all the more so because they were usually only sent during the infrequent launch windows where Earth and Mars came relatively close together in the heavens. The last time a launch had not happened according to schedule, there had not been an opportunity for another one for at least nine months, and nerves on Mars had become justifiably frayed during the resulting rationing of practically every resource on the planet.

"To the best of your knowledge?" Gromov asked. "Haven't you been receiving updates about it?"

"Normally I would," Westin said. She took a deep breath. "Something has gone wrong."

Every single person at the table tensed or fidgeted in their own way. Even Anguitine lost her stoic calm and blinked rapidly for several seconds. When you lived in an environment so extreme that even the air outside could kill you if you tried to breathe in it for too long (assuming the decompression didn't kill you first), the words "Something has gone wrong" took on a uniquely sinister meaning. They might be perfectly mundane on Earth, but here it meant something much worse than the cook burning the toast or the shower running out of hot water.

"What exactly has happened?" Takibana asked in a calmer voice than any of the others probably would have managed. That kind of thing was one of the reasons Westin had an ongoing friends-with-benefits relationship with him. He had a way of being soothing even when such a thing seemed impossible. It also made him a far better head of security than the last person who'd held the position. That one was now back on Earth, poor and destitute after all the financial sanctions thrown at him by the Syndicate after he'd let his job go to his head and beat up the cook's assistant for stealing more than his share of food. Takibana, while tough and willing to do things no one else would, at least never let things get that far out of hand.

"I'm sure I don't need to remind you all that nothing I'm about to say leaves this room?" Westin asked. Slowly, they all looked at each other and nodded. Not only did they know that, but most of them were even aware that the reminder was, in fact, very much needed. Both Takibana and Freelis had informed her of occasional tidbits of information circulating around Miranda that no one should know. Westin had her suspicions that Svensson was the one who couldn't keep his mouth shut, especially around those damned whores that he liked so much. In Westin's opinion, those three women on this planet were a mistake, but that was just one more thing that the Rothschilds insisted was important for the morale of certain elements. The prostitutes were, in Westin's view, exactly the same as this stupid table: a useless waste of resources for people with messed up priorities. The table, at least, could keep a secret.

"Fine then," Westin said. "All of you know that we very closely monitor what information from Earth reaches here." They all nodded again. Like the prostitutes, this was intended to keep the morale of the colonists up, but unlike the women, this was a tactic Westin agreed with. The people on this station had intentionally been drawn from all the walks of life on Earth, one of the many things the Syndicate did to give the impression that this was all one great endeavor to elevate the human race rather than just an attempt to corner the market on a super scarce commodity. The problem with having people from so many nations was that, at any given time, one of their countries or another would be going through some terrible crisis. Droughts, famines, wars, political uprisings. All these things were censored when any correspondence came through. The notoriously glitchy state of the colonies' v-mail services were not because of faulty equipment or atmospheric interference as the people were told. All messages in fact came through completely clearly. They just had people like Leah Hartnup and Suzie Kleinstock who would scrub information. Westin got the impression that Hartnup found what little of this work she had to do distasteful, so Westin gave most of the truly sensitive work to Kleinstock. It was for everyone's good, really. They couldn't concentrate on their own work and survival while they were worried about what might be happening on a planet over four hundred million kilometers away.

"Four days ago, reports started to come out of Siberia of some kind of sickness," Westin said.

"Why weren't we told about this?" Svensson asked.

"For the same reason we don't tell anyone else about the war raging through Malaysia or an earthquake in California or even when some famous comedian dies. None of you know the full extent of what happens anymore than the others because you all need to keep your heads in the games too. If you've got a problem with that, log a complaint with me in private after the meeting so I can properly tell you where to go shove it. I know what's going on back at Earth and whoever scrubs the information knows. You were all aware of this ahead of time, so I don't want to hear any complaints."

"No one's going to log a complaint," Takibana said, making a point to glare first at Svensson then at Freelis. Svensson lowered his eyes while Freelis glared right back.

"Four days doesn't sound like enough time for us to be worried," Gromov said. "Especially in Siberia. Far away from everyone else." She said it hopefully. If Westin remembered correctly, Gromov was from the city of Kaluga, which she believed was quite a distance away from Siberia. It still made sense, though, that she would be worried about a possible outbreak of something in her home country. Unfortunately, Westin wasn't about to give her any comforting information.

"What exactly do you mean by sickness?" Renner asked.

"Four days is just how long it's been since Russia let the rest of the world know about it," Westin said. "They kept it a secret up until the point where it spilled out of their borders and they didn't have a choice anymore. But from what little I've been able to get the Syndicate to tell me, it couldn't have started much earlier than that. It works fast. It's... oh hell. I can't remember all this. One second." She pulled a small datapad from one of the pockets in her jumpsuit and, after scrolling past all the daily reports and files and minutia of running Miranda, found the short file the Syndicate had sent her. Even that she'd practically had to beg for from Rochelle Rothschild herself. Apparently, the other two siblings had thought it best for Westin to be just as in the dark as the rest of the colonies and Rochelle had gone behind their backs. Westin had then called the meeting the instant she'd read the file.

"The WHO is apparently just now getting a chance to really study it. Their early reports call it a filovirus. That's the family it belongs to, I guess. They're calling it, uh, Bratsk after the city where they first positively identified it as a unique pathogen. Anna, am I pronouncing that name correctly?"

The superior definition screen clearly showed Gromov's face growing more and more pale. "Yes. That is close enough, at least."

"Okay, so what?" Renner asked. "There's a new disease. That happens all the time, doesn't it? It's not the end of the world."

Westin had to fight to keep her breathing calm and slow. She had to give everyone the appearance that she wasn't worried. At the same time, however, she needed the people in this room to understand exactly what was happening. "There are only a small number of known filoviruses in the world. All of them manifest as hemorrhagic fevers."

Pereira frowned and looked away as though that term rang a bell but he couldn't place it, which actually made Westin wonder about his qualifications as head science advisor. The only person who looked like she immediately understood was Anguitine, which Westin supposed made sense. In her previous career as a news network pundit, she had probably covered such things. Although she looked too young, Westin supposed she might have even covered the Marburg outbreak that had hit the Middle East about fifteen years ago.

"I don't know what that means," Renner said.

"Like Ebola," Anguitine said. "You all know that one, right? Just like that outbreak of Ebola back in 2014."

The rest finally started to look as shocked and worried as they should be, but Westin still had some bombshells for them. "There've been other outbreaks of Ebola since then of course. Including one a year ago."

"No there wasn't," Pereira said. "We would have heard…"

He trailed off as the significance of that statement dawned on him, and everyone in the room was silent for several moments.

Svensson broke the silence. "So you mean to tell us that something like this happened before and we were never told?"

"Of course not," Westin said, "especially since it was squashed fairly quickly. By now, treatments are pretty standard as long as the patients get medical attention quickly. The last Ebola outbreak only got as far as Brazil because it was a previously unknown strain and it took some time to adjust the treatments."

More quiet. They all had to be coming to the same conclusion (except poor Metzger, who still looked confused). It was just a matter of which one would voice it first. That turned out to be Gromov.

"There was an outbreak a year ago that you did not tell us about at all. Now you are telling us about one that only started a week ago."

"That's correct," Westin said.

"What exactly are we looking at then?" Pereira asked. "How bad is it?"

Westin went back to reading from the file on her datapad. "All attempts to hold the Bratsk virus in Russia failed. At first, the WHO claimed that was because the Russian government wasn't cooperating with them, but now all the countries it has spread to are cooperating fully and it still doesn't seem to be helping."

"How many countries so far?" Renner asked.

"As of the moment this file was sent to me two hours ago? Thirty nine. The majority of countries in Asia have reported cases, as well as Egypt and a couple in Eastern Europe. All international flights throughout the world have been grounded."

"That should be enough to stop it, shouldn't it?" Metzger asked. Westin shook her head.

"Apparently, this Bratsk virus is infectious before it even shows symptoms, and even then it only looks at first like a cold or flu. It appears to move faster than anything anyone has ever seen. Even if countries somehow prevented people from crossing the borders on foot, which is next to impossible for some of the larger countries, there's no telling how many infected people might have flown and to where before flights were stopped."

"Hemorrhagic fevers shouldn't spread that way," Anguitine said. "With Ebola or Marburg, people need to be exposed to bodily fluid like blood. The viruses cause people to bleed profusely and that's how they're transferred."

"Apparently this one is different," Westin said. "This one is airborne."

"We are not actually worried about this, are we?" Svensson asked. "The outbreak will come to a stop. It won't affect us here in any way. I mean, we are on a completely different planet."

Pereira glared at him before looking back to Westin. "There's a detail you haven't given us yet, Tasha. An important one."

"What's that?" Freelis asked.

"The mortality rate," Pereira said.

They all turned their attention back to Westin and stared at her expectantly. She had hoped they would come to the right conclusion without her, that she wouldn't have to say the facts. She knew, however, that most of them probably did understand completely. They were just holding out hope that it wasn't as bad as Westin had made it sound so far. As long as she didn't say it, the situation might not look so dire to them. That was the logic behind keeping things from everyone on every other occasion, after all. It wouldn't work this time, though.

"I'm going to say this just one more time," she said. "Not a single thing we're saying here leaves this room. We are going to spend the rest of this meeting discussing what to do next, but no one else can know, no matter what we decide. We can't allow a panic."

There weren't even any nods this time. Everyone just waited for her to continue.

"You have to understand," Westin said carefully. "If the current tactics used by the WHO work, this could all stop just as quickly as it started." She didn't add that it also required every single person who was infected to report their symptoms, and for them to do what they were told, and for them to keep from panicking and doing something stupid to further the contagion. Let everyone here have some kind of hope, just a little. "But that's just to contain it. Any other treatments they've used against other hemorrhagic fevers have been ineffective on this one. Current estimates say that just under half a billion have been exposed to it. And unlike with Marburg or Ebola, every single confirmed infection so far has reached to the hemorrhaging phase."

"So you're saying…?" Anguitine asked.

Westin nodded. "The mortality rate seems to be one hundred percent."

7

Just like every other room in Miranda, the cafeteria was cramped when it was completely full. There were supposed to be shifts for every meal, the miners and other essential personnel such as maintenance and custodians getting the first shift and more technical personnel, like Leah, getting the second shift. Today, it looked like several of the first shift had ended up on the second instead. The room wasn't supposed to hold more than twenty but Leah guessed the current occupancy was more like thirty. All three of the working girls were here despite formally being part of the first shift. This wasn't all that uncommon. Svensson wasn't the only client who kept them late, and often their only choices were the second shift or be forced to skip breakfast altogether. More noticeable was the handful of miners milling about, apparently with nothing better to do. Leah couldn't help staring at them and wondering what the hell was going on.

It was a rare occasion where Leah could get her meal and find an uncrowded table to eat breakfast in silence, if the reconstituted protein squares they passed off as eggs and bacon could truly be called a breakfast. Most of the time that wasn't the case, so she usually sat with Annabeth or Dr. Ruiz or either of Miranda's other two working girls. To her surprise today, though, there was still a whole table open that she could use for herself. None of the miners appeared to be sitting down except for Roy Osbourne, who had taken the seat closest to the food counter and was nattering on to the cook and his assistants. The other miners, all of them present, were standing together in the corner farthest from Roy and whispering to each other. Leah had the urge to go ask them what was going on, but she wouldn't have been surprised to find out they didn't know either. If Leah really wanted to know, she would probably have to go on a little creative fact-finding mission of her own after breakfast, assuming that she didn't have too much work to do. Or that she cared. She hadn't quite decided on that yet. It was probably nothing of interest beyond some mining equipment malfunction. She'd likely only look into it if she were sufficiently bored.

Even though the majority of other people on Miranda tended to look at meal times as the highlight of their day, to Leah it bordered on torture. The crowded cafeteria caused flashbacks to the times when she'd been a teenager in school trying to keep away from the constant torment of her classmates. It was remarkably different here, of course. They were all adults here and, although there were a few notable exceptions like Osbourne, everyone was more mature. It all still had a depressingly cliquish vibe, however. Most of the scientists stayed with the scientists. The miners stayed with the miners. Leah probably would have been happily accepted by the various computer and tech people if she had made the effort. Yet even among them she felt like an outsider. That wasn't because they had any problem with her, just that she'd been one her entire life and she didn't know or want to know how to be anything different anymore. She really just didn't want to open up to anyone and let them know any of her numerous secrets. Annabeth knew all of them and Martin knew most of them. That was about as open as she wanted to be.

Annabeth had stayed back at their room, opting to get some extra sleep and instead eat at lunch. That left only Martin, who was near the back of the breakfast line right now. That was good. She hadn't actually seen him in the last couple of days and she was starting to get anxious for a little alone time with him. Maybe they would be able to arrange something for later today, after she was finished with whatever computer and tech matters crossed her desk. As for him, unless he had something going on with one of his friends in one of the rec rooms later, Leah doubted he would be that busy. He was never busy, a fact he lamented about at length to her on a regular basis.

Dr. Martin Ruiz was part of Miranda's science team, one of the obligatory scientists the Rothschild Syndicate had sent to Mars under the pretense that they actually wanted to advance human knowledge of the planet. For most members of the science team, there were actually tests and experiments they could do with their time. The geologists especially were given plenty of funding and equipment, since the Syndicate was relying on them to either find more likely locations of diamonds on the planet or else find some other geological resource that would justify the Syndicate's continued presence on the planet should the diamonds ever play out. Martin, however, was a biologist on a planet historically known for being devoid of life. He could always use his expertise to experiment with microbes surviving on the planet's surface or something like that, but he wasn't given the same amount of funding. Honestly, the Syndicate didn't care much about what he did beyond simply being on Mars to make it look like they gave a shit. He might have had more to do if they'd stationed him in Kurtis to experiment with the crops, but Kurtis already had all the scientists they needed or wanted. So Martin was usually left to simply wander the halls of Miranda, only occasionally fiddling with some experiment in an effort to justify himself. It left him crotchety and cynical, which of course had drawn Leah to him instantly.

Despite the lack of Annabeth and Martin at the moment, Leah soon found that she wasn't going to be sitting alone today. Jeanette Weasel manifested herself from seemingly out of nowhere among the crowd and immediately plopped in the seat directly across from Leah. Karen Sulford, ever Jeanette's shadow, wound her way through the crowd a second later and sat next to Jeanette. Jeanette and Karen were the other two official working girls besides Annabeth, the Rothschild Syndicate's way of taking advantage of the lack of certain international laws on Mars as a way to milk even more money out of their operation. Jeanette, Annabeth, and Karen were all supposedly here of their own free will, having known exactly what their official duties would be, but just like the majority of other people on the planet, there had been certain loopholes in their contracts that ensured very little of the money they made would actually be in their pockets when they eventually returned to Earth. While Annabeth was prepared to accept it, Jeanette had decided early on that she wasn't going to have that. Leah liked to think of herself as one of the smartest and most resourceful people in the three colonies, but even she had no idea how Jeanette had gone on to be the number one purveyor of black market goods on Mars.

Even just looking at Jeanette Weasel (a name that, despite

various attempts at hacking into her files, Leah could neither confirm nor deny if that was real name or a mantle she had taken on herself) showed that she had access to things that shouldn't have been on the planet. For one thing, she wore makeup. She only used small amounts, what would have been considered subtle on Earth. But here, where the only people who officially had makeup were Westin and Anguitine for the various times they needed to do official videos to send back to Earth, it was downright ostentatious. She also had her hair colored black instead of its normal dishwater blond, and no matter how fresh the dye-job, she always seemed to miss her roots. It had taken Leah a while to realize that was on purpose, a subtle advertisement of her services - my hair is in fact dyed, and yours can be too for a price.

Everyone knew that Weasel was the one who could get you things, even the higher-ups, yet no one ever tried to stop her side business. Leah suspected that was partly because no one could prove she was doing anything against the rules, no matter how legally questionable some of her products might be in certain countries on Earth. More than that, though, Leah thought security was simply told to look the other way most of the time. She had no idea if anyone in management took a cut of Weasel's profits or if they were simply clients. Either way, as long as Weasel didn't get too bold, she was allowed to do her thing in peace most of the time.

As for Karen, Leah couldn't say the girl had ever made much of an impression on her. She was young, maybe nineteen or twenty, with dark skin, tight curls, and a London accent that was nonetheless hard to hear considering she mumbled everything she said. The only time Leah had ever seen her leave Weasel's side was when she was working.

"Hartnup, just the woman I wanted to see," Weasel said. "I've got a proposition for you."

"I'm good," Leah said. "How about you? Beautiful weather we're having."

"Oh don't act all hurt just because I didn't say good morning," Weasel said. "In fact, I'm betting you would have been even more annoyed if I had started out with idle chit chat. You would have thought I was wasting your time."

Leah shrugged. She couldn't exactly deny that. "Fine then. Buying or selling?"

"Little of both today," Weasel said. Her jump suit had been altered to have significantly more pockets than normal, and she reached into one just under her left breast. "Selling first. You're not going to guess what I have on this little guy." She pulled out a small black flash drive not much bigger than the tip of her thumb.

Leah sat up straight, all her attention now on the drive. "*Sorcerer One?*"

"Sorry, no. Not yet." Leah started to deflate, but Weasel made a hold-on gesture. "I'm telling you, I can get it eventually. You'll have that silly little game in your hands long before you leave. But this, this is something I just happened to get a hold of while getting something for someone else, and I knew you would pay top dollar for it."

Although she didn't want to be, Leah had to admit she was intrigued. "Well? What is it?"

"Guess."

Leah tried not to let her annoyance show on the off chance she might inspire Weasel to walk away with something she actually wanted. "How the hell would I know where to start?"

"I'll give you a hint, then. It's a show."

Leah dropped her utensils, which took a second to gently clatter to her tray. New television was rare on Mars. They only had so much bandwidth to work with sending data to and from Earth, and most of that was official business. A small amount of that was set aside for personal communication, no matter how edited Leah knew it to be. So for Weasel to have some new television show it meant she had either managed to get some time alone with the official communications relay, or else she'd had the little flash drive sent up physically at some point. Either way would have been practically impossible for anyone else to get, even Leah.

"It's not what I think it is, is it?" Leah asked, trying to keep herself from getting her hopes up.

Weasel smiled at her. "Only if you think it's the Thirty-Sixth Doctor's complete three series run."

Leah let out an involuntary screech of glee before she physically covered her mouth with her hands. A couple of people around them glanced their way for a few seconds before going back to their own business. Everyone knew to let Weasel conduct her business in peace if they ever hoped to use her services again.

Leah immediately forced herself to calm down, thinking about exactly how much such a thing would cost her. The only form of currency used here between individuals in the colonies was Rothschild scrip, and everyone only got so much to work with every week. If they wanted more, they could trade in some of the Euros they were supposed to get upon their return to Earth, but at an exchange rate that was distinctly unfair to everyone involved except the Syndicate itself. And yet Leah got the impression that Weasel had an almost supernatural feel for economics and would somehow come out of this all rich, even if most of her wealth was in scrip. She was too savvy to put all her eggs in that one incredibly fragile basket. She had to have some way to convert the scrip back to Euros or dollars, or else why would she even bother?

"Alright, so hit me with the price," Leah said. She was already reaching for her plastic timecard and PDA in her pocket, getting ready to do the complicated process to set the specific amount to transfer and from where. She knew the price would be steep and she could probably just wait the nine or so months it would take before she was back on Earth, but she was bored out of her skull lately and, although she had never in her life thought she would say this, getting into computer systems that she shouldn't be was getting old.

"Twenty thousand."

Leah stopped reaching. "You've got to be kidding me."

"Don't tell me you can't afford it. I may not know your exact pay rate..." She looked around at everyone around them to see if anyone was listening, then leaned closer to whisper. "...but I do know they don't just get someone out of prison unless that person has the kind of skills someone's willing to pay handsomely for."

"You've never charged me anything like that before."

"I've never had anything I knew you wanted this badly before. The others around here, usually they're pretty easy to satisfy. Especially the guys. That part of my job may be a touch on the distasteful side, but it's almost always quick, if you know what I mean. You, however, I've always known to be more careful. So I made sure I found something you wanted and saved it for the right time."

Leah thought she suddenly understood and brought her hands away from her pockets. "So it's not really money you want at all, is it?"

"If I could get that out of you too I figured that was a bonus. You're right, though. There is something I want more from you. A service, if you will."

"If someone's trying to use you as a way to sleep with me, you'll just have to suck them off yourself," Leah said.

Interestingly, it was Karen who seemed more offended by that than Weasel. "That's not nice."

"You just ignore her, sweetie," Weasel said. "She didn't mean it." She leaned over and gave Karen a peck on the forehead, a gesture that wasn't so much sexual as it was motherly.

"Sorry," Leah said. "But seriously. What do you want?"

"What I want is to use some of your skills and know-how."

"Which ones, exactly?"

"The ones used to erase certain aspects of incoming communications."

Leah stiffened. "I don't know what you're talking about."

"You know, most people around here seem to think the most important commodities I have to sell are physical goods. It's not. You know what is more important? Information. I know a handful of things I shouldn't, and that's exactly what allows me to do the rest of my business. And one of the things I know is that we don't actually know everything we're supposed to. One of the other things I know is that you're one of the two people responsible for that."

Leah wanted to say something, but nothing would come out of her mouth. Her job here required a lot of things. Mostly she maintained computer systems, although the Syndicate knew well enough to keep her away from the most important systems and gave them security she wasn't supposed to be able to crack. She did programming when it was needed, mostly for anything that was both automated and nonessential. But the only thing she actively despised among her duties was going through people's personal messages and redacting information. She was good at it, her v-mail edits near seamless, yet it violated her moral code. If the Syndicate didn't hold so much over her head, she would have refused outright. She considered it a minor victory that she didn't have to do all of it, although she wasn't sure exactly who else they had working on it. There weren't a lot of other candidates, but there were a few.

"You don't have to admit it," Weasel said. "That's okay. It's enough that I know. And I also know that makes you the one who would most likely know how to restore said communications."

Leah looked down at her tray and speared some of the vaguely egg-smelling protein block with her fork. "I suppose I'm listening, but you've got to know I can't guarantee anything."

"That's fine. Here's the job. I was just given a v-mail, although I'm not telling you from who until you agree to do the job. Client privilege and all that. Real simple message. Doesn't look like anything special. But he just got it a couple hours ago and now he's really worried about it. I don't think he knows a lot about computers or v-mail. He just thinks it was corrupted or something. He's completely clueless that someone messed with it on purpose. So he came to me thinking that with all my resources I might have some way to 'clean it up.'"

"And if I don't do this, what are you going to do, tell everyone that I've been censoring their personal messages?"

Weasel looked honestly hurt. "I would never blackmail you or anyone. That's a morally shitty thing to do. And even worse, it's tacky. No, I'm not telling anyone. If you don't do it, you don't get this little guy, simple as that." She waved the drive a couple times then slipped it back into its pocket. "I know there's someone else that does the censoring, but I'm not completely sure who. That's one little bit of information I don't know yet. I suppose that if you know I might be able to make it worth your effort?"

"Sorry. I'm not really sure."

"Can't blame a lady for trying. Either way, I'll figure out a way to get my client what he wants. It's just any way other than you will take more time, and he was rather insistent that I get results quickly. He's willing to pay a lot more than I think he can actually afford. Going to be trading in for an awfully large amount of scrip, and that's even after I decided to give him a discount."

"A discount? You? Feeling generous all of a sudden?"

"Nope. Feeling curious. I'm sure I'm not the only one who thinks something weird is going on this morning. Would I be right?"

Suddenly, all thoughts of the Doctor and her latest transformation slipped away in favor of Leah's own curiosity. "You think whatever was erased has something to do with the stopped mining?"

"Maybe, maybe not. You have to admit this is highly weird. When was the last time they stopped mining for anything short of broken equipment? Yet I overheard a few of the miners saying everything was working as far as they knew. Hell, when someone gets hurt they don't even allow the mining to stop any longer than it takes to get the body out of the way. Of course, if you were the one that censored this particular message you could just tell me and you wouldn't need to restore anything."

"Wasn't me. The last one I cen… uh, it just wasn't me."

"Either way, are you up for this?"

"All I can promise is that I'll try. You know, sometimes I think you guys don't have a real good idea about what exactly I can and can't do. I'm not some hacker from a big-budget Hollywood movie."

"Sure you're not. Just like I'm sure you're not just covering your tracks so you don't have to betray your beloved Syndicate?"

Leah's grip tightened on her fork. Some deep part of her wanted to bury her fork in Weasel's hand just for suggesting she had that level of loyalty for the Rothschilds. Luckily, she liked Weasel just well enough not to do anything like that. The Syndicate had gotten her out of prison, but the environment they had placed her in was only slightly better. She got access here to computers, something she was actually banned from on Earth, but in prison at least she'd gotten food that actually tasted like food and she didn't have to worry about the world outside trying to kill her. Every other person on the planet, as far as Leah knew, was here more or less by their own volition. Leah, on the other hand, had never been given much choice.

Weasel must have realized she'd nearly crossed a line, because she didn't push it any further. "Stop by my closet when you're done with your breakfast," she said as she stood up from the table, taking her breakfast tray with her. "I'll have the v-mail for you."

"And the *Doctor Who* episodes?" Leah asked.

Weasel wagged her finger at her. "Not unless you can get the job done. Pleasure doing business with you." Karen got up and followed her as she weaved her way back through the crowd as it thinned out. Most of the colony was on its way to their various jobs by now, and Leah would have to do the same shortly.

Before she could give much more thought to Weasel and her task, Martin came through and sat down next to her. "Hello," he said in his thick Brazilian accent. "Sorry I took so long. I had to wait for Barkley to make more bacon." He gestured at a square on his plate that only resembled bacon if someone were to squint and ignore the smell. He leaned in for a kiss and Leah gave him a quick peck on the mouth. Martin probably would have preferred more, but Leah had never been comfortable with public displays of affection. Where she'd grown up, people would have looked at her with scorn for kissing a man. Just because things were different here didn't make her any more at ease with it.

"Can't stick around," Leah said. She shoveled a huge helping of the so-called food in her mouth.

Martin frowned. "I've barely seen you for days."

"I've got to get going," Leah said. "I need to go see Dr. Lipschitz before I punch in."

"Something wrong?"

"I just wanted to make sure he has enough of my hormones to last until the supply ship."

"You don't need to be paranoid about that. They wouldn't have kept you supplied all this time just to let you run out right at the end of your time here."

"Still. You know me." She ate the rest of her breakfast in as few bites as possible, hoping that her stuffed face would hide any signs that she was lying. Yes, she had been paranoid that something would go wrong with her supplies after all this time, even if the Syndicate had been more than accommodating of her medical needs. But she wasn't so worried that she actually needed to check. She just wanted the time to get that v-mail so she could fix it, give it back, and get her goddamned *Doctor Who*.

Although, she had to admit, she was just as curious as Weasel. She wanted to know what was going on, even if it turned out to be nothing. The curiosity was killing her.

The meeting was over, everyone was gone, and Westin sat in her office leaning back in her chair staring at the ceiling. With the room to herself, her fingernails were back in her mouth where she worked on a particularly troublesome thumbnail that had been bothering her for the whole meeting. If she chewed on it for much longer, she would probably start bleeding at the cuticles, but it was either this to calm her nerves or take some of the pills she had in her lower desk drawer. In truth, her nails weren't calming her nerves in the slightest, but the THC pills would dull her senses too much. They were one of the few perks of her job, provided to her by her superiors even though the substance was technically not supposed to be on Mars in the first place. Half the time she never took them herself, instead trading them to Weasel for favors, but they tempted her now with the promise of a temporary buzz that would keep her from showing everyone just how scared she really was.

She wouldn't touch them, though, at least not for now. Maybe before bed tonight, even if the day promised to be longest she'd ever spent on Mars. She just had to keep reminding herself that she was no stranger to pressure. She'd handled much in the last five years on this dusty red ice-ball of a planet, and she could handle just a little more until this all blew over.

Because it had to blow over. She was sure of it. The only other option was that the Bratsk virus would sweep like wild fire all over Earth and they would be stranded here, no help, no more supplies, no contact when things got too out of hand.

Nonsense, she thought to herself. *That's not going to happen. It can't happen. A virus can't simply wipe out all human life. That sort of thing only happens in fiction.*

Paranoids and the mentally ill could talk about the Apocalypse all they wanted, but that wasn't the way humanity worked. There were always survivors. In fact, it wouldn't even come to wondering about survivors. The virus would be stopped in its tracks before it reached any truly civilized parts of the world. She was sure a number of people on the colony would have a problem with her saying their homelands weren't civilized, especially Gromov, but that was beside the point. The virus would be stopped before reaching Europe and the United States. Countries like that wouldn't be taken down by something so tiny it could only be seen with a microscope.

Still, she had to make sure the colonies were prepared for any eventuality, whether there was a real threat on Earth or not. She could sit here and try to be as optimistic as she wanted, but it was being a realist that would keep these people alive. It had in the past, whether the colonists knew it or not. She thought back to Max Perrish, as he had been known on Mars. The Rothschild Syndicate had very exacting background checks in place for anyone who wanted to become part of their grand endeavor, but Max, like that horrible Osbourne character currently in mining, had slipped through the cracks of their psychological profiles. She'd tried to send both of them back to Earth, but the Syndicate had insisted that would be a waste of resources. Osbourne had so far proven not to be a problem and, despite his general unpleasantness, Westin had started to think she'd overestimated his issues to start with. Not Perrish, though. No one had realized how psychotic that guy was until he had killed someone during a fight over shoelaces. It was only then that the Syndicate had dug deep enough into his records to realize he wasn't Max Perrish at all, but Louis Maxwell Murphy, wanted for the murder of his girlfriend two years before he had found his way to Mars. It still remained a mystery to this day how he had crafted a new identity capable of fooling a group as powerful as the Syndicate.

As far as the people of the colonies knew, Max Perrish had been sent back to Earth. Most of them were unfamiliar with orbital mechanics or exactly how travel to and from Mars had to work. They were just told that an emergency craft had been sent up while they were sleeping, sending Perrish back to Earth to be properly tried for his crimes. They didn't need to know that there was no launch window around that time and no way to keep him safely locked up until there was one. After all, the tiny jail they did have was designed more for the occasional petty theft or disorderly conduct and wasn't even a true punishment next to that person getting their pay docked. Instead, Perrish had been the first and so far only person executed on Mars.

Westin had passed the sentence herself and, as much as she had wanted to turn away, she forced herself to watch as Takibana had pushed him into an airlock and depressurized it. The only other people who knew what had happened were Renner, who had needed to approve the location in their gardens where Perrish's body had been used for mulch, and Bindi Gruber, the poor security guard that had been in the wrong place at the wrong time and was forced to help them break down the body.

She could have let him live, Westin supposed. There might have been ways to deal with Perrish that wouldn't have troubled her sleep at night. But they only troubled her a little, because in the end she believed that he would kill again. Even if he didn't and they had found a proper way to lock him up, including some way to send him back to Earth that wouldn't put anyone else on the ship with him in danger, she still hadn't been willing to waste valuable resources on filth like that. Every piece of food he got was something that no one else would have. Every precious and rare particle of the air he breathed could have gone into someone else's lungs. As much as she had agonized over that choice, she had always understood that it was no choice at all.

And if those were the kind of choices she needed to make now, then she was prepared. She'd already discussed some of them with management, but there would be many more tough decisions she might need to make before this was over, and for right now she needed to anticipate as many as possible and decide well in advance what course of action she would take.

Westin stopped biting her nail and pulled out the PDA she'd been carrying around in her pocket. Most of the computers throughout Miranda were linked, if not physically then wirelessly. While the Syndicate might have neglected certain things like proper environment suits for the majority of the populace, the computer systems at least were state of the art, with new components and software sent to Mars on a regular basis. Different people installed different parts and software but no single tech person ever had everything. It was a system implemented specifically with people like Leah Hartnup and Suzie Kleinstock in mind, people who had been recruited because they were the best regardless of any criminal past. Even if they teamed up (and their psych profiles determined that they would both be disinclined to such an action), there were other fail safes to keep them from doing any mischief. Kleinstock, based on Westin's interactions with her, probably wouldn't do anything. She was still too awed by the fact that she was even here, and her crimes had been limited to doxxing a couple of low-level celebrities she'd decided were misogynists. Hartnup was more of a troublemaker, but the Syndicate had information over her head regarding Hartnup's part in major bank account hacks that would go to the authorities if she stepped too far out of line.

All those precautions, however, still weren't enough for the Rothschild Syndicate. Firewalls, highly secure passwords, blackmail, and psych profiles could all fail to do their jobs, after all. That was why the most important information of all in Miranda was only kept on one of three PDAs: one that Westin kept with her at all times, one that belonged to Metzger, and one in a thick, secure safe hidden under the rug in Westin's office. They could only be updated through hard line connections twice a day. Even then, unbeknownst to Metzger, Westin didn't even give his PDA all the relevant information. She knew he was the weakest link in this scenario, especially now when Westin wasn't sure if he could hold up under this new amount of pressure. Metzger would come in later, on an exact schedule as always, to get his PDA updated and the file Westin downloaded for him would be missing most of the relevant information. If Metzger had ever realized something was off in the past he had never said anything. In fact, Westin doubted he ever even looked at the thing. He only ever carried it because it was protocol, and he would die before violating protocol.

Westin turned on the PDA and swiped through the area where she kept her confidential reports to start typing up her notes and thoughts about the meeting they'd just had. One of the most important things they had all decided was that, on the surface, nothing would look like it had changed. This was no longer just about keeping a dangerous mining operation running smoothly, it was about keeping panic from reigning in a tight, fragile environment. If the Bratsk virus turned out to be a worst case scenario of wiping out everyone on Earth, or even just wiping out enough people that they could no longer provide proper support to the colonies, then there were any number of ways the colonists could act, most of them dangerous.

So normal operations had to continue. In retrospect, Westin thought it was a bad idea that they had suspended mining operations for the morning. If they did become cut off from Earth then mining would be rendered irrelevant. Not only did it do nothing to contribute to their survival, but it also sapped their resources in potentially dangerous ways. Small amounts of air were lost to minute imperfections in the airlocks, energy expended from batteries in the environment suits could be used elsewhere, and above all every unnecessary trip out onto the surface could result in an accident that meaninglessly lost a life. Svensson in particular had been irate about that particular tidbit, although he refused to say why in front of the others. Westin knew he made the working girl's he employed on a regular basis use his emergency escape hatch rather than be seen coming and going from his apartment, a practice Westin had always disagreed with but had been approved for him personally by Kurtis Rothschild. Westin was happy that she could finally override that, even if she herself didn't think much of the working girls to begin with.

But all talk of unnecessary long walks on Martian wastelands aside, Westin judged that for the moment there was more potential danger in the miners not doing their duties. Already there would probably be whispers around Miranda that something was off. Nothing else could change until they got further information about what was going on back on Earth. Nothing on the surface, at least.

The rest of the meeting had been had been dedicated to figuring out what they could discreetly do to improve their chances of survival in the event of a prolonged disconnect from Earth. There had been plenty of ideas bandied about, yet few of them could be executed without the colonists understanding something was wrong. Although they had food production at Kurtis, it had never been intended to serve all one hundred and fifty plus people on Mars for extended periods of time. They still relied on continuous resupplies at regular intervals. The upcoming supply ship would help immensely, but Renner would have to have some of his tech people run some mathematical models to determine how far that would take them all. In the meantime, the smartest thing to do would be ration any and all available food, but again, that would be noticed and questioned.

That had been the point when Westin had ordered anyone on the management team with private food stocks to relinquish them back to the colonies. Most of the management had nodded quietly, but Svensson had protested, blabbing on about how he had earned his eggs and fresh tomatoes and whatnot, that this was an outrage and nobody else had worked for it, yadda yadda yadda. Westin hadn't even bothered trying to reason with him about the greater good. People like Svensson didn't see any good greater than the good they could do for themselves. Takibana had stepped into the conversation with a couple of vaguely threatening words resulting in Svensson finally relenting. Westin would have to keep an eye on him. If public food supplies started to dwindle suspiciously, she knew whose apartment to check first.

Conserving energy and air had also been suggested, although those weren't quite as dire. The two were even linked in a small way, with oxygen generators converting water to their base components of oxygen and hydrogen. The hydrogen could then be used as a fuel source in a pinch, although it was so volatile they wouldn't dare use it in most circumstances. Instead, excess hydrogen was stored in containers kept separate from the main buildings where it would wait until it could be combined with oxygen that had been taken from carbon dioxide scrubbers to make water again. There was also a small amount of breathable oxygen produced by the greenhouses in Kurtis to supplement their supply. They might start worrying if the colonies were cut off for an extremely long period of time or there was a catastrophic loss of atmosphere within any of the colonies, but more likely air wouldn't be an issue.

Energy likewise looked good. Some power was drawn in from a massive number of solar cells atop all the buildings and in arrays near each colony, although they had to be cleaned on a regular basis in order to be useful because of the commonplace dust storms. The majority of the power, though, came in through Rochelle, which sent it to Kurtis and Miranda through three conduits buried just below the dusty surface. Rochelle took a twofold approach to providing the other colonies with their energy needs. The first was the reason it was so far out from the other two colonies in the first place, the geothermal power plant. This was the most sophisticated plant of its kind, more experimental and more efficient than anything that had ever been tried on Earth. The first colonists at Rochelle had needed to drill deep into Mars' crust, deeper than anything that had been attempted on Earth, purely because Mars' geological structure was very different. While Earth had a thin crust with thick mantle and core, Mars' crust was the thickest part while the molten inner space was much smaller. In most parts of the planet, geothermal energy likely wouldn't have been possible, but here in Tharsis, so close to so many long-dormant volcanoes, geological surveys had found places where the planet's molten innards were closer to the surface.

The other source of energy was nuclear. While the average colonists often seemed squeamish about getting their energy this way, the small nuclear power plants that made their home on Mars were a safer source than others like. The very first landers for the colony, the ones that had arrived even before the humans, had used small fission cores and state of the art shielding. These stayed in the original landers, which were then hooked into the power grid. In terms of radiation danger they posed to those outside, they were actually less dangerous than walking around in environment suits on the planet's surface where the lack of atmosphere and planetary magnetic field allowed in enough radiation from space that it would kill most unprotected life.

There was some possibility that the colonies might have problems when it came to water, according to Martin Freelis. The man was in charge of anything and everything to do with $H2O$ ranging from its production to their handful of attempts at finding water anywhere on the planet. There were water plants at the other colonies but the majority of their operations were run through him in Miranda. According to Freelis, there would likely be a point in the future, given enough time, where water would be a problem, but not because there wasn't enough. The water plants had a ninety-seven percent reclamation rate, a fact Freelis was justifiably proud of, and the various methods at producing it helped make up for the remaining amount and gave them a surplus under the best of circumstances. The problem, according to him, was that those circumstances would be far below optimal if they lost regular supply drops. The technology they used to keep the water clean was prone to wearing out. For a few people at a time, which had been the original plan when most of these technologies had been designed, this would not have been an issue. For one hundred and fifty-six people, though, he estimated the gray and black water produced by the colonists would outstrip their ability to clean it in just over a year.

So Westin had issued a general notice throughout the colonies that a water embargo was on, with water only to be used for drinking and waste disposal. She ordered these from time to time anyway when there were maintenance issues with the water systems so it wouldn't look too outside the ordinary, but the embargo wouldn't make much difference in the long run. Already most cleaning was done through chemicals. Those chemicals, too, would start to become scarce after so long, but they weren't as important just yet and Westin could wait to worry about them until she understood more of what was going on.

Beyond these most pressing issues, there wasn't much more Westin could have done at the moment. Maintenance crews would be given orders to step up their inspections of the colonies' radiation shielding and any other vulnerable aspects. The exercise areas of each colony, usually required for every colonist to use on a rigorous basis if they didn't want their bodies to atrophy in the low gravity to the point that they could never return to Earth safely, would be down for "repairs" so people weren't using up their own valuable excess energy as their rations were quietly cut.

All of these things were nothing other than stopgaps, Westin knew. They were temporary measures like sticking fingers in the holes of a cracking dam. None of these measures would likely matter if they were cut off from Earth permanently. Under those circumstances, every single person in these colonies would die.

"That's not going to happen," she whispered to herself. It was a mantra she expected to repeat to herself often the longer this crisis continued, even if she knew there were always going to be too many factors here that would be completely out of her control. She'd learned that early on in her life being the oldest of seven children. Chaos had always reigned, it had been her duty to lessen it as much as possible when her irresponsible parents hadn't been up to the task. Once they'd grown up, half her siblings had hated and resented her for being controlling. The other half had recognized how shit their lives would have been otherwise. Westin had never expected all of them to understand, but all seven of them had survived their childhood. She knew she was the one responsible for that, so it didn't much matter if half of them had disliked her tactics.

As she was ruminating on this, the monitor on her desk chirped that it had received a message. Westin turned it on and accepted the v-mail to see Rochelle Rothschild at her trademark black walnut desk, her suit perfectly pressed and clean, the very picture of absolute professionalism as always. Her face, however, showed Westin a side that she doubted Rochelle ever let the rest of the world see. Her skin was pale and lacked any makeup, which was just as well because Westin didn't think there was enough makeup in the world to cover up the thick dark bags under her eyes. Someone had made a basic attempt at styling her hair, but here and there strands of platinum blond had come undone and hung at the edges of her face. Rochelle seemed to neither notice nor care about these. Her hands were folded in front of her but her shoulders were slumped, a posture Westin had only seen her in once before, during that ugly business several years back between the Syndicate and the DeBeers cartel.

"Westin," Rochelle said in introduction, then appeared to think better of it. "Tasha."

She paused for a moment as though she expected Westin to say something back. Not that such a thing was possible unless someone eventually managed to figure out faster than light communication. Still, Westin said hello. It was a long standing ritual between them.

"I miss you," Rochelle said. Westin gave a wan smile, kissed the palm of her hand, and then placed the fingers lightly on the screen over Rochelle's cheek.

"Tasha, I'm sorry if the previous v-mail was a bit brief and the file I sent you was short on details. It was the best I could do on short notice before I had to run off to the next meeting. I'm stuck in Stockholm right now, since I was here meeting with some buyers when all the flights were shut down. Kurtis and Miranda are both back in the States trying to keep everyone else in the Syndicate as calm as possible. I don't think they're assuaging anyone's fears, though. Everyone is spooked. The stock market is falling. Economies all over the world are taking a sudden nose dive. So naturally all either of them can think about is how hard this is going to hit profits. I get the impression that both of them think this Bratsk thing is being blown out of proportion."

Rochelle stopped, staying so completely still for several moments that Westin thought perhaps the v-mail had glitched and was stuck on one image. Then Rochelle's breath hitched.

"I don't think it is, Tasha. Here in Sweden, we're supposed to be far enough away from all the outbreaks that the local government is telling us not to worry, but I've seen footage of some of the hospitals along the border filling up. I think it's still managing to make its way through despite the precautions.

"I've got to tell you, I'm scared. Stupid, huh? Considering how many assholes I've faced down since taking charge of the Syndicate, I shouldn't be afraid of something as small as germs anymore. I kind of wish you were here. You know as well as I do how hard it is show the world you're stone-cold when on the inside your shaking. Hell, I bet that's kind of what you're feeling right now. I can't even imagine what it has to be like up there, knowing what's going on down here. It could be easier if we could face it together."

Westin wiped away a tear. She hated seeing Rochelle like this. She may have been dressed as one of the richest and most powerful women on Earth, but all Westin could see when she looked at her was a scared little girl. For a moment, she forgot all about her worries here on Mars and went into that matronly mode that she had honed as a teenager. All she wanted to do was hug Rochelle and tell her everything would be all right. If she could do that, it might even make Westin forget that she wished someone could do that for herself as well.

Rochelle looked down at her hands for several seconds, taking deep breaths, then looked back at the camera. The little girl was gone again, leaving only the businesswoman who somehow convinced NASA and the United States government into giving up any claim they might try to make on a diamond operation worth trillions of dollars. It had probably helped that the Rothschild Syndicate had right around the same time generously donated enough to single-handedly get the government out of all debt.

"Enough of that bullshit, I suppose," Rochelle said. "I'm sending you another file with this message including everything I can possibly fit regarding what is known about the Bratsk virus and the situation it's creating. I figure you might need to be aware of what countries are currently affected and how that's all playing out politically. I'm sure you're keeping it as quiet as possible up there but just in case you aren't for some reason, you'll be able to tell your people how their homes are faring. I don't know why you would do that but I trust your judgment." She paused. "If something happens to me, Kurtis and Miranda probably won't be as forthcoming with you, so I'll continue to send updates whenever I can."

She stopped again, this time looking several times like she was going to say something else and then stopping herself.

"Tasha," she finally said. "Just... take care of yourself." Rochelle reached forward abruptly and the message ended.

Westin stared at the blank screen, sometimes smiling and sometimes frowning. She supposed she needed to look at any further data Rochelle had sent her. That was what a responsible leader with over a hundred and fifty lives in her hands should do. Sometimes, though, Westin was tired of being a leader. Sometimes she just wanted to be normal person. So she started watching the message again, telling herself it would only be this one more time.

Three times later, she finally stopped.

9

Mikhail Svensson had earned everything he had and more. That was what so many of the people who surrounded him didn't seem to understand. Coming from a small village in Sweden, a village so small he liked to say he hadn't seen traffic lights until he'd been fourteen (when really the city had a population of nearly a hundred thousand people), no one had ever helped him on his climb to becoming production manager on the first off-world mining colony. He'd done all of this on his own. So what he had, he deserved. The respect of his peers in the meeting earlier? He'd developed that through nothing but hard work. That woman in his bed this morning? His by right.

So it baffled him completely that the lowly men of his mining crew, men who could never hope to get to Svensson's lofty position, didn't respect him. None of them would come out and say it to his face, of course, considering that with nothing more than a word from him and they could be on the next transport back to Earth where they would live out the rest of their miserable lives wondering how they had so royally screwed up their best chance to be something. But he knew. He could see it in the way they looked at him, the subtle changes in their voice when they spoke to him. Osbourne was the only one who ever seemed to give Svensson his due, and that wasn't saying much considering what a miserable worker he was. Even Davis, who barely ever said anything beyond pointless platitudes and generic life stories, somehow managed to show Svensson his disdain.

Svensson watched them now from his control room over the main mining airlock, making sure that none of them went out of his sight. They knew he was watching and he sensed instinctively that even now they were trying to figure out ways to screw him over. He could tell from their posture and the way most of them kept their backs to him so that, with their bulky environment suits on, he couldn't see the subtleties of their faces. He listened intently to anything and everything they said through the coms in their suits as they talked to each other, trying to figure out if they were using some kind of code to talk behind his back. Or maybe they were mouthing the words to each other where he couldn't see, although he didn't think any of those lowlifes were smart enough to think of that.

No, none of that is right, Svensson thought to himself. *You know it isn't*. Intellectually, at least, he knew it wasn't. Yes, he was sure they hated him, but no, it wasn't like they were plotting anything. They couldn't. They were too lowly to even conceive of such a thing. They were just schmucks, a word he had only recently picked up in English but had taken to using even when speaking in his native Swedish. It captured the essence of most of the people on this planet in a way no other word could.

Whatever they were, Svensson knew he would need to keep himself in check around them for the rest of the day. He was aware he had a tendency to see motives that sometimes weren't there. The emphasis, however, was on the word *sometimes*. Just because he was paranoid didn't mean the world wasn't after him. He couldn't remember who originally said that. Some singer probably, although it didn't matter who. It was still true.

That was exactly why Kurtis Rothschild had selected him for this position. The two of them had met nearly twenty years ago when Svensson was just coming up from a minor arm of the Syndicate and Kurtis was only just out of his teens and trying to find a way to prove himself among his siblings. Saying they were friends would have been wrong, since Kurtis wasn't the kind to make friends. But he was the kind to be able to see someone and truly find their potential. In Svensson, by Kurtis's own admission, he had found the perfect person to act as production overseer in certain mining operations. He hadn't minced words, either. The words "jumpy" and "paranoid" had been repeated often. Those were exactly the qualities he was looking for, though, when it came to workers handling tiny rocks that were worth millions (or billions, once Svensson had been transferred to Mars) of dollars.

Preventing theft was actually easier here than it was at any of the mines Svensson had supervised on Earth. To start with, the environment suits only had a couple pockets, all of which Svensson had security check every time the miners came back in from the frozen crater outside. Secondly, there was nothing these people would be able to do with them even if they did somehow get a few diamonds past Svensson. It wasn't like anyone here in Miranda could cut them and then wear them. The diamonds were just useless rocks in this environment until they got back to Earth and could be sold, and all miners had their belongings thoroughly checked on a regular basis to ensure they weren't somehow going home with them. It was a perfect system, one that Svensson himself had put in place.

That didn't stop the occasional miner from trying, of course. In the early days, a pair of miners had almost gotten away with it, one doing the actual stealing while the other would have just been the mule, since he was on his way back to Earth already. Security had been less willing to obey Svensson at that time before he had successfully convinced them that this was an honest problem. The mule had insisted he had nothing to do with it, that he didn't have any clue how the diamonds had ended up in his belongings, but after a v-mail to Kurtis Rothschild, Svensson had been able to make sure that the miner would get the proper punishment from the Syndicate once he was back on Earth. As an added security measure, the diamonds were sent back in their own transport to insure no one would be able to break into them on the way back. That had been Svensson's idea and had gone on to save the Syndicate a great deal of money since the separate transports didn't need to be outfitted with life support systems. Svensson still had the printed out commendation Kurtis had given him for that on the wall of his apartment, right over his bed where his many partners could easily see it.

"So what do you think it was?" one of the miners said in French through the coms. Svensson wasn't sure which one, nor did he care, although from the accent he guessed it was one of the Indians.

"Svensson's probably listening in right now. You could ask him," someone else said. That one might have been York. Svensson knew that the rest of them saw York as one of their leaders, which to Svensson was about as big of an insult they could possibly have given him. Svensson was and would always be the one in charge no matter how much York might want to usurp him.

He'd been thinking of some way to get some kind of revenge on York for that slight, although after a couple years he was still trying to figure out some way to do it without getting himself in trouble.

Svensson pushed a button on his control panel that allowed him to speak to them all at once. "Ask me what?"

"What that was about this morning," someone else said. Another Indian accent but a different voice. Dip. Svensson only knew that one because he was the one that had given the boy his nickname. It was a lot easier to say than whatever the hell his real name was.

"That's none of your concern," Svensson said. In fact, he was pretty sure it wasn't anybody's concern. So there was a panic on Earth. It didn't matter and no matter how much Westin and the others wanted to prepare for some horrible eventuality, he knew nothing would come of it. The important countries wouldn't get a virus that was wiping out all the minor ones. That was simply the way reality worked.

From his window in the control booth Svensson could still see them as small, like gray lines against the red dustbowl of Poynting Crater, yet that wasn't how he normally watched them. The mining operation itself had gotten far enough from the airlock over the years that the only effective way to watch them without a camera would have been to follow them out into the harsh, almost atmosphere-less landscape. Svensson had worked hard in his life to get above that kind of work. Instead, he saw them all through a series of monitors to his left, where their helmet-mounted cameras gave him a view of whatever they were seeing. The cameras weren't quite good enough that he could see their expressions through their tinted visors, but he could still see the way they paused at his words. He wasn't quite sure what that meant, but he knew it was probably something he shouldn't like.

"Sir, it's just that—" Dip started to say.

"You should all be working, not talking," Svensson said. For a moment none of them moved, a fact that irritated him to no end, and he searched over his control panel for something to yell at them about. "The number two drill is slowing down by eight percent. Why aren't any of you on that yet?"

"I will take a look," one of them said. Svensson neither knew nor cared who. He just wanted them to get back to work. It was bad enough Westin had halted operations this morning, and he didn't want them to get any further behind just because these people wanted to stick their noses where they didn't belong. He wouldn't be surprised if they were even doing this on purpose just to make him look bad.

One of the miners went up to drill two and opened an access hatch on its side. The drill was mounted on a six-wheeled apparatus similar to some of the earlier rovers like Curiosity, making the entire thing the size of a compact car. The drill was underneath it, still working and sending up a small cloud of red and gray dust nearby. As the miner started to punch a few buttons on a keypad, Svensson chimed in again. "What are you doing?"

"Sir, I have to stop it first if I want to do any…"

"No stopping. You can run diagnostics while it's still going."

"I don't think that's very safe," Dip said.

"It's safe enough. Just do it already."

The miner performed the diagnostic, albeit much slower than Svensson would have preferred. Between the eight miners, there were six pieces of equipment currently with them out in the crater - two drills, two drones searching the area for the higher concentrations of diamonds, and two rovers whose jobs were to comb through the detritus left from the drilling and sort the diamonds from the crap. Since the robotic vehicles did most of the work, the miners could basically laze around for most of the day, no matter how much they might try to make noise about their working conditions.

There was a seventh rover out there just beyond the current field of activity, the Venture rover itself, but none of the miners went near it and Svensson didn't have the same remote access to it. While the Rothschild Syndicate had purchased massive amounts of earthbound equipment from NASA and the other space agencies of the world for use in their operation, the Venture had fallen through a number of legal cracks. Now it sat dead as a part of the landscape, slowly gathering heaps of red dust, since the operation that had controlled it from Earth had itself been integrated into the Syndicate.

Svensson stared at it for a while, idly wondering how it might positively affect the mining operations if they could have access to it. Unfortunately, it was still technically United States property and would likely continue to be as long as the US suspected it might need a claim to this land. They didn't make a stink about the Syndicate's presence purely because they had been paid off and paid handsomely, but the time could always come where they might change their minds. Until then, it had to stay unmolested unless the Syndicate wanted to declare itself hostile to the US. Svensson had already been given the proper access code to the Venture by Kurtis, which he himself had charmed out of a certain high-ranking NASA official over a roaring fire and a bottle of champagne, just in case the time might ever come where they could use it.

The rest of Poynting Crater, for now, was empty. The Miranda colony and the mining operation around it only took up a portion along the southeast rim. From end to end, Miranda was only about a kilometer long, spread out only because it was easiest to build in modules that didn't need to go up or down the slight incline at this point of the crater. The main portion of the mining operation itself, here at the southernmost end, was as far as possible from the administration wing, with the various living areas in between. In theory, should the diamonds continue to be found throughout the crater, Miranda could eventually become a whole round city surrounding the cash cow in the center. Svensson liked that idea, especially the possibility that he would still be the one in charge of production at that time, but that was far off. And it was even further every time someone freaked out on Earth like now, thinking that their petty problems should trump their operations here. It made Svensson sick and angry.

"It looks like there was a minor jam in one of the waste rock chutes," the miner working at the drill said. "I think it fixed itself, but I'd really like to turn it off and take it back to the shed for a checkup, if I can."

"You can check it after your shift is over," Svensson said. "We're not wasting any more time."

"Would I get paid for that?" the miner asked.

"It's after your shift. What do you think?" The miner didn't say anything back, which pleased Svensson. Eventually these men would give him all the respect he truly deserved. For now, though, he would just have to take every little victory he could.

10

Leah hadn't gone directly to Weasel for the v-mail after breakfast. She hadn't even reported to her tiny work cubicle right away, despite the stringent rules colony management usually kept in play regarding employee work times. She had learned long ago, for people with the right skills that the Syndicate wanted to keep happy, the concept of work hours were malleable. As long as she did at least seven hours of official work a day and kept accurate records of the time, she was allowed some latitude in when exactly that work was done. In theory, she could work at night and sleep all day, similar to Annabeth's schedule, if she really felt the urge, but she didn't need to go that far. What she did need to do was make sure she got her time in at the workout room, and the hours immediately after breakfast were usually ideal for that. She'd had the room all to herself except for the janitorial and maintenance staff cleaning and greasing the equipment.

While there was a tendency by some to think of the workouts as not important, it was actually official Rothschild policy that every employee get at least forty minutes logged in the workout room every day. In one way, it was considered a sort of preventative maintenance against poor health, considering there were a number of medical conditions that were simply too costly to take care of millions of miles away from a real hospital, but even more so a workout routine was essential for any and every person who ever wanted to go back to Earth. Leah was more conscious of her body and its needs than most, so she always put in the extra effort to keep herself toned and ready to return to a planet where the gravity would try to crush anyone who hadn't put in the work and kept up on the supplements that prevented their bones from weakening. With only so many months left, she'd been pushing herself even further, knowing that no matter what she did, she would still spend an unfortunate amount of time recovering when she got back.

Following that she had gone to Dr. Lipschitz to get her daily dose of hormones (a detail she kept hidden from everyone but

Martin and Annabeth, telling anyone else who got curious that she needed regular treatment for an unspecified gastrointestinal issue) and then went on to Weasel, finding her in her quarters. Weasel hadn't let her go without trying to interest her in a few extra things like contraband chewing gum, THC pills, nicotine patches, or a disturbingly large silicon dildo. Leah had thought better than to purchase or ask the origin of any of these things, instead just taking the drive with the v-mail and getting out of there before Weasel tried to tempt her with anything else.

That finally left Leah just before lunchtime with the v-mail at her cubicle. There were other things that she was supposed to be doing today, with new security programs to prevent theft from the medical center being on the top of her to-do list, but after sitting at her computer for several minutes imagining the latest adventures of the Doctor, she decided to just say screw it. As far as she was aware, theft from anywhere within the facility itself was rare. She'd found references in a few forbidden files about attempts to steal drugs once or twice, but given the brutality of some punishments around here most people wouldn't have risked it, instead going to Weasel if they really wanted some kind of illicit meds. The kind of things they had Leah working on most of the times were busy work, anyway. She would do whatever she could on the v-mail before lunch then give it back to Weasel. By early afternoon, she could be sneaking time on her computer to watch Doctor Number Thirty-Six and her companion before moving on to her real work. All in all she was prepared for it to be a rather lazy day.

By the time she finally looked at the clock on her computer and realized it was 16:30 hours Rothschild standard time, she had to admit that she'd stumbled into something a lot more complex than she'd expected when she'd woken up this morning. Of course, Leah was very much aware of the Rothschild Syndicate's tendency to censor the news from Earth, given her occasional part in such things. She was also aware that Westin and Metzger and anyone else in management knew better than to let her see any of the truly sensitive materials. She'd always assumed they didn't know, however, just how easily she could find those things out if she really wanted to. Or how badly she had to fight not to want to.

Putting her in charge of these kinds of things was like forcing an alcoholic to work as a bartender. In a partially full brewing vat. Under a waterfall of beer and whiskey. Because that was how she had unwittingly found herself on Mars in the first place.

Leah had been fascinated with anything and everything involving computers from an early age, from the very moment that she had realized that she hadn't fit in with her peers and never would, that they would never see her the way she saw herself. Computers didn't have that same level of judgment. They were beautiful on the outside but even more exquisite underneath when someone truly looked at them, their components, their code. They were something she could look deep into the same way she wished others would look into her, beyond the clunky and inexact surface to something more fitting underneath.

Beyond that, she had been even more fascinated with what she could do with them. With every new generation computer technology grew more complex and providing more ways to exploit and use them, no matter how hard anyone tried to close any holes they might have in their security. In her teens, this had translated to breaking into her parents' computer and discovering, to both her horror and her intrigue, that they had a thriving side business broadcasting themselves having live sex to paying customers. She'd never told them she found that out. Instead, in what she told herself was her just payment for having to look at that, she set it up so that fractions of every payment they received went into her own savings. By her mid-twenties, she had turned to exploiting the security systems of banks, usually small time but larger when they were careless enough and she thought she could get away with it. Eventually some of them had caught on and she'd ended up in prison, where the Rothschild Syndicate had found her. They'd liked her ability enough that they'd pulled the necessary strings to get her here, and had even been comfortable supplying her extra medical needs. The best person to design the computer security on their most sensitive project, they'd decided, was someone who already knew all the illicit tricks and therefore could prevent them.

In theory, this left her in the perfect position to exploit everything, but in addition to the further info they had on crimes she'd never been prosecuted for, there must have been something in the psych eval they'd done that showed how badly she wanted to put that all behind her. It wasn't so much that she wanted to use her skills for good as it was that she was bored with using them for ill. It no longer provided any challenge or thrill, and she'd eaten enough terrible swill in prison and here on Mars that she wasn't eager to go back to any of it once she was done. No, as soon as she was back on Earth she had every intention of finding a place in Wales far from people and... well, she wasn't entirely sure what her plans were for the long run. She just knew that a life of any kind of excitement was a young person's game, and she just didn't have it in her anymore.

Repairing damaged video files, however, wasn't her usual area of expertise. She'd thought she'd be able to get something purely because the process she used to censor v-mails in the first place wasn't that sophisticated. All she did was enter garbage data into the image and audio at key points. The original information should all still be there, at least in the ones she typically did. After all, other than her and Kleinstock and one or two possible others, no one should have even been able to recognize that this wasn't just a natural occurrence caused by background radiation or storm interference or whatnot, let alone know how to fix it.

So it had surprised her that, upon her first playback of the v-mail, there wasn't just static or blocky digital corruption hiding the pertinent information. Instead, it looked like whole sections of the video had been snipped out, with only brief moments of black in between. That probably would have required actual video editing software, not just the quick and dirty fix she used. Leah didn't even have access to that kind of software. Only Diane Anguitine, perhaps, would have had any need of it on Mars.

Leah sat back and replayed the v-mail multiple times, listening to it on her ear buds so no one in any of the other cubicles would realize she was up to anything unusual. Not that they would have bothered her anyway. There were only four other spots in this room, and other than Kleinstock, none of them would have known what to make of what she was doing even on a normal day. And Kleinstock, strangely, didn't appear to be here at the moment.

Okay, so I can't just restore it, she thought to herself. *What else can I do to get those damned episodes?* The v-mail played through again, and for the first time Leah started to wonder what exactly could have possibly been on this video that had warranted these kinds of measures. It's not like there would have been any deep secrets on here. Although she had never spent much time with any of the miners, her minimal impression of this Sandeep guy was that he was a polite, relatively quiet man that kept his head down and did his work with few problems. There shouldn't have been anything truly important in a v-mail to him.

Maybe if I actually know what the hell this guy is saying, I can start to piece something together, Leah thought. So far she'd been listening to it only in the original language, which she couldn't even positively identify by name, let alone speak. She'd run a quick translation program on it that identified it as Marathi and then shown a rough English translation at the bottom of the screen, except that hadn't given her much more to work with either. Although the translator seemed to mess up the grammar at many places, she was at least able to figure out that this guy on the screen was Sandeep's brother-in-law and most of the discussion seemed to revolve around his pregnant sister and her... morning sickness maybe? The translator seemed to have problems with that part. The v-mail cut off abruptly at the end before the brother-in-law could go into any more details. That was probably the part he had enlisted Weasel's help to fix. He expected more to be there that could give him more information about her condition. Leah found herself oddly moved by that level of care and commitment to his sibling. There would probably be another v-mail at some later time if only he were patient, and then he would get his info, but he was worried enough that he had to have it now. Having never had any siblings in her life, she found that kind of dedication foreign and odd.

While he was likely fixated on getting more information out of that ending, however, Leah was more interested in various parts from the middle of the message. Although it was difficult to be certain when listening to a language she wasn't that familiar with, the brother-in-law's words seemed oddly clipped in several areas. Going back and repeatedly looking at those areas specifically, Leah began to get the impression that some of the things he'd been saying were cut out. Yet it was a spectacularly well-done job. She had to expand the video as much as her software would allow and watch in very specific, minute areas to see places where his fingers or the folds on his clothing jumped at each cut. This was far more effort than she had ever put into any of her own attempts at obfuscating events on Earth. It was even, as far as Leah was aware, a much deeper effort than she had seen Suzie Kleinstock ever do in the past.

And all over a man talking about his wife's morning sickness?

By the time Leah realized she had missed lunch and was on her way to missing dinner as well, she had become absolutely convinced that there was something far more important and disturbing going on here than she had first suspected, but she didn't think she was much closer to finding out what exactly it was. She was starting to get the impression that maybe this had something to do with the mysterious shutdown of operations this morning, although that was little more than a hunch with no actual evidence to back it up. One bit of evidence she did have, at least, was the timing of the cuts: they all seemed to come when the brother-in-law was discussing his wife's symptoms, or where she was being treated. She'd also poked around the file a bit longer, hoping there was something in it she thought she could pull out, but this was no longer in her area of expertise. If she were some fictional hacker, she probably would have been able to spout some nonsense about the source code and get the answers. Instead, if she really wanted to continue pursuing this, she would have to find other ways.

Of course, that left the question of whether or not she actually wanted to keep going. Her natural curiosity and distrust of authority wanted her to dig deeper, to make sure she knew the answers purely because someone else didn't want her to. Ten or even five years earlier, she wouldn't have hesitated. Now, however, she was so close to being done with Mars and Miranda and the Rothschilds. Now was not the time to poke the hornet's nest. There was no telling what the powers that be might do in retaliation if she discovered some truly horrible secret. A bunch of *Doctor Who* episodes were not worth losing all the money she had earned here, or worse, suffering some unfortunate "accident" on the way back to Earth.

No, she decided. She wasn't going to get involved. It was probably nothing anyway. The edited footage probably alluded to some unrest in India or something like that, something that really didn't matter on Mars but they just wanted kept quiet for the sake of morale. She'd give the drive back to Weasel, say there was nothing she could do, and maybe try to barter for some other cheap way to get those episodes.

She stood up from her chair and stretched to crack her back, taking notice of her environment for the first time that day. The large level of autonomy the Syndicate afforded her meant she didn't have to worry about anyone ever coming to her cubicle and watching her work over her shoulder, but the office area still had people going in and out at all times. There was one other person in another cubicle, a man Leah recognized as the head custodian (even if Leah always had just a little trouble remembering his name). Even his job keeping everything clean and in working order required a disturbing amount of paperwork and Leah often saw him around here at this time of day frowning at something on a computer screen as he hunted and pecked the keys.

Something was missing though and, given what Leah had been listening to and staring at for the last several hours, she was surprised it took her so long to realize what it was: Kleinstock still wasn't here. Leah frowned as she went over to Kleinstock's cubicle to look for any sign that she'd even been here at all today. It was difficult to tell, considering how tidy she kept her space. Leah thought back through the rest of the day, trying to remember if, even while she was so focused on her problem at hand, she had heard or seen any sign at all of Kleinstock coming or going. While she usually tuned that kind of thing out, Leah suspected she would have remembered that today. She might have even tried to cautiously get her to open up about what exactly she had excised from the v-mail.

Against her better judgment, Leah went over to the custodian's cubicle, taking a moment of pride when he looked up at her looked at her chest instead of her eyes. She absolutely understood why most women had a problem with the constant male gaze but, considering how much she had hated her body for a good portion of her life, she was happy when someone else saw the beauty in it, no matter who it was.

"Hey, uh…" She panicked for a moment, still drawing a blank on his name before she finally saw the nametag on his jumpsuit. Leah had ripped hers off within her first few days on Mars and sometimes forgot that not everyone had the same violent reaction to being labeled in public. "David. Bechdel. Whichever you prefer…"

"Only my friends call me David," he said, then looked her over again. Okay, that time she had to admit it was a little creepy. She suspected that he was the kind of guy who wouldn't be undressing her with his eyes if he knew the truth about her. "You can call me Dave."

"Dave, I'm…"

"Leah Hartnup. Just because you can't be bothered to remember my name after we've both been here for five years doesn't mean I don't remember yours."

Leah flushed. She did have to admit that even with so few people on the planet she'd never put much effort into knowing many of the people. Especially the ones that she, admittedly, thought of as below her.

"Uh, I'm… sorry about that." Dave gave a noncommittal grunt and went back to frowning at his screen.

"Dave, I don't suppose you've seen Kleinstock at all today? She's the…" Leah stopped herself. If he knew who she was, then he probably knew who everyone else was as well.

"She's gone," Dave said, not bothering to look away from his screen this time.

"Gone? What do you mean, she's gone?"

"Gone as in not here."

"Well yes, but… I mean, where else is there even to go?"

"Miranda isn't the only colony on the planet, sweetheart. Last I checked there were two others."

"She's at one of the other colonies? Do you know which one?"

"Wasn't my day to keep track of her."

"So you don't know?"

"Of course I know. I see and hear everything around here. People will have sensitive conversations around me and not even realize I'm something other than the furniture."

"Pardon me if that sounds a bit exaggerated."

"Say it's exaggerated all you want. Doesn't change the fact that I know what you and Kleinstock do when you're not programming things."

Leah paused, unsure of whether to acknowledge anything. Dave looked up at her long enough to give another one of those creepy glares. He had a big bushy moustache, and in that moment Leah realized he looked exactly like someone out of a vintage 1970's porno.

"Relax. I never tell anybody anything I know. All the deep dark secrets of the three colonies would have gone back with me on that transport back to Earth."

Leah suddenly found herself very uncomfortable with this whole conversation. It was time for her to put something in her poor neglected stomach anyway, but she still hadn't gotten the information she'd wanted in coming to talk to him. "So which colony did she go to? And why?"

"Saw her getting put into the shuttle for Kurtis right after breakfast this morning," Dave said. "As for why, well, I just work under the assumption that anything I don't know everyone will find out eventually."

Which, Leah realized, was not the same as him saying he didn't know. She just didn't think she was going to get anything more out of him for now.

"Right, well, thank you," she said. He grunted a reply as she turned to go for the door, not bothering to even look at her, but when she turned around one last time she found him staring again.

She went out into the hall and away from him as quick as possible, stopping just outside the door to think again. So Kleinstock was actually gone from the colony. Leah wasn't sure what they intended to do with her at Kurtis, but the timing was too suspicious to simply be some kind of emergency computer work, especially since the specialized needs of Kurtis and Rochelle required computer techs of their very own. No, Kleinstock had not left Miranda for any legitimate work reason, Leah knew it. She had been moved because whatever she knew was something the powers that be did not, under any circumstances, want getting around Miranda. There was no way this could be anything other than temporary, however. This wasn't Earth. Someone who knew a deep dark secret couldn't just be put into a witness protection program on the other side of the country. All of this was highly curious and disturbing.

I thought you were going to drop all this? she thought to herself. Well, that *had* been her intention, really, but this new little piece of information was too much. She knew herself better than to believe her need to know wouldn't fight her now tooth and nail.

So I guess I've got to go with it, she thought. She made her way in the direction of the mess hall, her mind already planting the seeds of a possible plan.

11

Annabeth knew that her family, or for that matter the rest of society, disapproved of her profession. Prostitution (she knew that no one else on Mars called it that, but she was a big proponent of saying what she meant and not hiding behind bullshit) was taboo for a reason, after all. It was very easy for people with power to use it to control others, to treat them as less than human. And yet so many of those so-called "worthwhile" professions were just as demeaning. While she might get treated like a plaything at night, there was something to be said about having her days be little more than leisure. After collapsing into her own bed, she'd slept until lunch time, then got her lunch and spent the rest of the day doing only what she wanted.

Granted, it wasn't like there were huge numbers of things to do here that could occupy her time. While Leah was working at her computers and the miners were outside toiling in one of the harshest environments humans had ever lived in, Annabeth spent her days reading anything and everything she could download from Miranda's digital library. There were also a few craft projects she'd gotten materials for from Weasel, although she didn't do those too often. The cramped confines of her apartment with Leah were not the best place to be messing around with sewing needles, sequins, and glitter. Still though, the monotony aside, Annabeth appreciated the life she led here. If it meant letting sweaty guys like Svensson stick body parts into certain places during the night then she could live with that. Hell, back on Earth she would have been doing that for free.

Still, she was at heart a deeply social person and all that free time while most of the other people on the planet worked could get to be too much. Annabeth had long ago come to enjoy and wait for the sounds of Leah just outside the door, keying her code into the door panel to come in. While it was difficult to tell sometimes how Leah felt about their friendship, considering how quiet and brooding she could be to Annabeth's typical bubbly and exuberant mode, Annabeth personally felt that Leah was less like a roommate and more like a sister. Even if Leah could sometimes get on her nerves (more because that was inevitable in such cramped confines than because of any personality conflicts) with her grumpiness and thousand-yard stare, Annabeth recognized that she was the yang to Leah's yin.

When Leah finally did come back, Annabeth was wearing nothing but a blue robe and pink fuzzy bunny slippers (again courtesy of Weasel, and Annabeth couldn't even begin to comprehend where that woman had gotten these, although they were worth every penny). She expected Leah to see her get-up when she came in and shake her head as always, partially because of the absolute ridiculousness of it and partly because Annabeth had managed to go through yet another day without putting on proper clothes. Instead, Leah walked in quietly, her head down and her lips moving silently as though muttering a problem to herself that only she could hear.

"How was work today?" Annabeth asked. "Hack any mainframes? DDoS any servers? Partridge any pear trees?"

She expected either a smile or an exasperated sigh. Instead, Leah closed the door behind her, went over to plop (as much as one could plop in low gravity) on her bed, and then continued to stare at her feet.

"Leah?" Annabeth asked. "Leah. Hey!" She walked over to Leah and snapped her fingers in Leah's face. "Mars to Leah. Come in. Over."

"Oh. Uh. Hi," Leah said. She still didn't look at Annabeth though. Instead, she stood up and went to the room's one viewport. Annabeth wasn't sure what she expected to see. There was dust rising from the mining site and probably would be until sundown since Svensson was probably going to work the miners extra long to make up for the mysterious delay this morning. Annabeth had no idea what any of that had been about and hadn't much cared either. All it meant to her was that Svensson probably wouldn't be back in time to get an appointment with her tonight. That was fine by her. She was going to need to get dressed soon and make her way to the request boards to see who, if anyone, she was going to be with instead. In theory, she had a choice and could reject anyone she wanted. In truth, though, if someone made too many requests for time with the working girls without eventually being scheduled in, they had a right to file complaints that the working girls weren't doing their jobs. In the end, Annabeth and Weasel took turns with a few of the less savory clients. Both of them agreed that they'd rather not force those kinds of people on Karen. She tended to be a more delicate person.

Of course, the earlier delay also meant that none of the miners themselves would likely be asking for her services tonight either, and for all she knew whatever had caused the delay would keep others away as well. As much as she liked the occasional nights off, she didn't get paid anything for them. If she left here and didn't find any requests for her services, she might just have to go around soliciting, and that just tended to make everyone involved uncomfortable. When people put in a request, it just felt like a standard part of living and working on Mars. When she had to convince people to join her it felt like… well, like prostitution.

"Soooo, did you eat yet?" Annabeth asked. "According to the menu, Barkley's supposed to be making his version of Nashville hot chicken again, but after the problems with the bathrooms after last time I hear he's going with spaghetti or something instead tonight."

That finally elicited a coherent response. "His spaghetti always tastes like mush," Leah said.

"Everything he makes tastes like mush. The only time it doesn't is when Alvarez is the one doing the actual cooking."

Leah finally looked at her and seemed to take in what Annabeth was wearing. "Did you even leave the apartment at all today?"

"Why would I? Well, I guess I did go get lunch, although no, I didn't wear this. I was surprised I didn't see you there."

"I was busy. I was looking at…" Leah paused again, and Annabeth thought she had trailed off permanently for a moment. She was in one of those deep introspective moods that usually meant Annabeth would have to eat dinner alone again. Maybe that would be okay. It would give her time to think about who might not have spent any quality time with her in the past few weeks. Come to think of it, Annabeth didn't think Alvarez had come to any of the working girls to relieve her stress of working with

Barkley recently. Maybe the two of them could…

Her thoughts didn't go any further as Leah interrupted her. "I think I might need your help."

Annabeth stood straighter. "Anything. You know that."

"I don't know if you've noticed it or not, but something very, very strange has been going on all day."

Annabeth shrugged. "I guess. I don't know. Other than the work stoppage this morning, everything has seemed pretty normal. Except…" She stopped, thinking back to that morning.

"Yes?" Leah asked.

"There was the way Svensson acted this morning. Did I even tell you about that? He got some call and it seemed to fluster him."

"What was it about? Did he say anything specific?"

"Uh. No, I don't know. Maybe. I was kind of distracted trying to get my clothes back on. Why? What else has been so strange?"

Leah explained what she had been working on all day, starting off her typical quiet self but getting more animated the deeper she got into the mystery. She finished off the story with her conversation with David Bechdel, making sure to add in how much he had creeped her out. Annabeth held her tongue on that. One of the unexpected aspects of her job was that she saw a side of people most others never did. Bechdel may have come off as creepy and a little womanizing in public, enough so that pretty much every other woman in Miranda hated being around him. Annabeth, however, knew him to be shy and gentle in the bedroom. That didn't excuse his act in public, but it kept her from actively being disturbed by him.

"Okay, sure. That's all very weird and disturbing," Annabeth said. "But what do you expect me to do about it? Just go around using my charms to ask random people if they know what the administration is hiding?"

"No. Not random people. If they're so keen on keeping whatever this is a secret, I don't think most of them would appreciate that approach. But just one or two people? People that maybe you could, uh, you know…"

Leah looked for a moment like she was about to make some kind of awkward obscene gesture. Annabeth saved her the trouble.

"Just because I can give a mind blowing orgasm or two doesn't mean anyone's going to give me privileged information, you know."

"Mind blowing orgasm, huh?"

"Yep."

For a moment, the expression on Leah's face shifted back and forth between disgust and intrigue before she became serious again. "I didn't expect anyone to just give you anything useful. I was thinking something else."

"What then?"

"Using your ability to get into certain personal quarters and then getting any relevant information you could find."

"What, you mean like stealing?"

"You're not actually stealing if you don't take anything physical. There would be information on PDAs or flash drives or something like that. All you would need to do is look at it and then come back and tell me what you saw."

"Still sounds close to stealing."

"I told you, it's not stealing."

"And stealing is against our code."

"Code? What code?"

"Our code of ethics. Or honor. Or whatever you want to call it."

"Who's this 'our?'"

"You know, us. We, those of us whom…"

"Wait, wait, wait. You seriously mean to tell me that prostitutes have a code of honor?"

"How the hell should I know? It's not like I was ever involved in the life back on Earth. I mean the three of us, me, Karen, and Weasel. There are rules."

"And stealing's not allowed?"

"Not from our johns, at least. Honestly, who the hell knows how Weasel gets some of the stuff she does, but not a one of us would take something from someone who has paid to be with us. There's a level of trust that can't be violated."

"Wow. Okay." Leah paced back and forth through the room for a couple laps. Annabeth got out of her way, not wanting to interrupt her. Finally, Leah stopped again and turned to Annabeth. "So what exactly are you saying you would be unwilling to do?"

"No taking of anything. No breaking into anything."

"Not even computers?"

Annabeth was getting annoyed by this line of questioning. "Look, don't take this the wrong way. You know how much I love and respect you. But I'm not a hacker. I don't view other people's privacy the same way you seem to. I'm not judging you or anything regarding what you do or what you may have done in the past. But you don't have the right to ask me to do it. It's that simple."

Leah nodded and went back to staring at her feet for several seconds. When she looked back up she had an expression Annabeth wasn't sure she liked. "So there's nothing I could do to change your mind about that?"

"No, not about those two things."

"No stealing, no breaking in?"

"That's right."

"But if someone else just so happened to do that while you were, oh, I don't know, occupying someone's time?"

"Oh God, Leah. Really? Come on, you can't expect me to be a part of this."

"What if this is important, Annabeth? I mean, they made someone disappear rather than let the truth out. On a planet that only has just over a hundred and fifty people."

"You're making it sound like they Jimmy Hoffa'd her. They just sent Kleinstock to another colony. That's not even close to the same thing."

"Do you really mean to tell me you don't want to know? That you don't think this is important at all?"

Annabeth thought for a moment. She didn't have Leah's relentless need to know things she wasn't supposed to, but she would be lying if she said she wasn't curious. She just wasn't sure if curiosity was enough to get her to go against what she believed was basic decency.

"Leah, I'm not sure…"

"If you do this for me I'll owe you. Big time. Especially when we get back to Earth."

"But I'm not going back for a couple years yet."

"Doesn't matter. I'm not the kind to forget a debt, you know that. And you know what I can do. Come on. You know how useful it might be to have someone like me owe you a favor. I could get information you might want, I could quietly delete criminal records…"

Annabeth smiled. "Except I know you would do that for me already."

"You're right, I would. And all I'm asking is that you do something similar for me."

She stopped smiling. Annabeth wasn't sure at all if she was comfortable with this. Sure, for all she knew this was important. Or it might have just been some kind of clandestine Rothschild business, some manner of corporate chess game that she didn't want to be a pawn in. For certain she knew she didn't want to violate her personal code for this. There were more than enough people, both here and back on Earth, who thought that just because of what she did for a living she was the lowest form of human scum. All the more reason, in her mind, to conform to some kind of higher code. That way, no matter what anyone else might see when they looked at her, Annabeth at least could look at herself in the mirror.

At the same time, though, she didn't want to disappoint Leah. They had been there for each other throughout all their time on Mars, each of them looking out for each other, being there when some john treated Annabeth like shit or when Leah had some scare that others outside her small circle of trust might discover she was transgender. It didn't feel right for Annabeth to say no to this. She certainly knew that Leah would never say no, no matter what Annabeth might ask.

"If I say yes to this, then you owe me big time," Annabeth said.

"Absolutely. Anything you need, anytime."

"So what are you going to have me do? Or, I suppose I should say *who* are you going to have me do?"

"Well, there's a few things I hope you can tell me first," Leah said, and they started to lay out a plan.

12

At the moment, Westin was once again alone in the conference room. She'd had visitors coming through almost constantly throughout the day. This wouldn't have been too unusual on any other day, so she hoped no one noticed that most of the people coming and going hadn't been the typical mid-level administrators but various security officers.

Takibana had been in the most, giving updates on various precautions Westin had thought to set in place in the event that the news about Earth did indeed get out and cause a panic. On more than one occasion, Westin had felt the incredible urge to just take Takibana back into her office where they could release some of their pent up fear and uncertainty, but Westin refused to lose focus. Maybe they could do something like that later. Hell, maybe she would just skip Takibana altogether and go for one of the working girls, although she hadn't done that in years. The last time had been when Karen Sulford had first ended up on the planet, and it had been obvious before either of them had even taken their clothes off that the girl had been scared out of her wits from the idea that her first trick on Mars would be the most powerful person on the planet. Westin had told her to leave and paid her anyway. Ever since then, the idea of using those particular resources for herself had made her feel itchy inside, and she would rather they would just leave the planet entirely.

None of these thoughts had anything to do with her current task, though. While she might have been physically alone in the room, she was not the only person talking. Both of the view screens on the walls showed Renner and Gromov, each of them looking worse for wear. Renner's complexion was pale and his face glistened with dampness. He'd been exerting himself only moments before this, but Westin wasn't going to ask in what way. Gromov somehow managed to look even worse. She had thick bags under her eyes like she'd gone several days without sleep despite the fact that she'd only learned what was happening to her homeland this morning. She also sniffled repeatedly during the conversation, making Westin think that she might have recently been crying. Westin couldn't blame her, although she hoped this wasn't going to cause problems with what they needed to talk about and do. Gromov right now was the perfect example of why no one else could know yet or, under the best of circumstances, at all. There was still a chance that this would all blow over, although the continued reports she was receiving suggested otherwise.

"I need a report on Kleinstock," Westin said. "The signal from the transport said it arrived safely."

"She hasn't given us any trouble so far," Renner said. "For the most part."

"And what exactly do you mean by that?"

"I mean she's petrified. She's your news scrubber, after all. She's got some idea of what might happen to people who are sent to Kurtis. People you might want to disappear."

"Wait," Gromov said. "What does he mean?"

"He doesn't mean anything, you didn't hear anything, and neither of you are going to bring up that particular line of inquiry again, understood?"

They both nodded, although Gromov reluctantly so.

"You told her that she's completely safe, right?" Westin asked Renner.

"Sure, I told her that as long as she keeps her head down and doesn't try to speak to anyone she'll be fine, except she doesn't believe me. Was this really a necessary precaution, Westin? This seems like the kind of thing that's going to come out eventually anyway. Why use the extra resources to transport her all the way here?"

"You ever been married, Renner?"

"Me? Uh, no. I was engaged to a guy for a while, but we broke it off."

"I've been," Westin said. She held up her left hand close to the camera so he could see the groove on her finger where the wedding band had once been. She'd been divorced long enough that the groove should have disappeared by now, but she had continued to wear the simple gold band for long after she'd been separated. "Imagine that one of the two people in a married couple has an affair. Do you think that it's going to be more destructive if the faithful partner finds out about the cheater sooner or later?"

"I don't know. Is this supposed to be a trick question?"

"Yes, in that it doesn't matter. The affair is going to be destructive no matter when the other person finds out. There's no way to stop that. There might, however, be a way to mitigate that destruction if the cheater tells the spouse about it all on her or his own terms."

"You're losing me here, Westin."

"What I mean to say is that we control the flow of information here. We are going to hold onto that information for as long as we can, just in case this all blows over. And if it doesn't, then we enact a carefully worded way of releasing that information."

"But why?" Gromov asked. "That is what I still do not understand. We are talking about grownups, not children. They can handle any information we give them."

"And keeping it from them is only going to make things worse when they find out," Renner said.

"Excuse me, but who's in charge here?" Westin asked. "You two or me?"

Neither of them answered. Westin could tell from the looks on their faces that pulling rank here was not the best option. She might have been in charge here but only because people back on Earth had declared it that way. They, on the other hand, were many kilometers away and each controlled essential resources required to keep everyone in Miranda alive. Rank in this case had to be tempered with reason and being right. Or, if nothing else, with enough charisma to make them think she was right.

"Between the three colonies, we may be an incredibly small community, but that doesn't mean we're short of rabble-rousers and just plain paranoid assholes. You can thank the Rothschild selection process for that. If they'd gone with the stricter psychological qualifications that NASA and other space programs used to use, we might not have that problem. But we do. Out of the fifty-eight people currently living in Miranda alone, I know of at least three ex-cons and two who actually failed their psych evals but made it to Mars through nepotism and cronyism. I could pull up the statistics for your own colonies as well, but I'm sure I don't have to. You both know your own people well enough to realize there's a few troublemakers. Am I right?"

She took their silence to mean that she was.

"So what happens when some of these people hear that we may just be cut off from Earth? What if someone starts questioning the rationing of food and decides they need to horde it for themselves, or even use it as leverage to get what they want from others? And those people who failed their psych evals? What if they find out that everyone they ever knew on Earth is in danger or, God forbid, already dead or dying? Are either of you truly prepared to clean up suicides? How about security? What if someone decides they no longer have anything to lose, maybe trying to get a guard's weapon or perhaps just killing someone they don't like?"

Westin stopped to take a breath, noticing that Renner had grown quiet and thoughtful. Gromov, on the other hand, was harder to read.

"We are millions of miles from any environment that could even remotely be called hospitable, and even that may be filling with a deadly virus as we speak. We have to prepare ourselves for the possibility that after that last supply drop that's on its way, we might be alone. Maybe temporarily, maybe permanently. Thousands of things could go wrong, and all it would take to destroy us all is one. I have a duty to protect these people. *We* have a duty to protect them, from any threat. And right now the greatest threat, the one variable that could tip everything to complete chaos, is our people themselves."

"But… what if the supply drop has the virus as well?" Gromov asked.

Westin paused. She hadn't thought of this possibility yet, but now that it had been presented she had to consider it. Yes, there was a possibility. The rocket that had launched the supply ship had been in a part of India that hadn't shown any signs of the Bratsk virus yet, but the latest reports had shown that the virus had indeed shown up there soon after. Westin couldn't say that just now, though. In the same way that she needed to keep the truth from most to prevent a panic, she also needed Renner and Gromov confident that everything was under control. Westin would worry about the possibility of an infected supply shipment later. After all, they needed those supplies if they wanted to continue surviving. There was no way to avoid them.

"The virus needs a human host to spread it," Westin said. That certainly seemed like the case based on what she had seen so far, but she had no way of knowing that for certain. "And the supply ship as it currently stands doesn't have the level of life support needed for anything to survive on it." Again, that was just an educated guess. Gromov, however, remained stoic and hard to read. Westin wasn't sure if she liked that. If she had been crying just before their call then a sudden shutdown in her emotions couldn't be good.

"I guess the question comes back to Kleinstock, then," Renner said.

"Treat her well," Westin said. "She did everything I asked of her and she doesn't deserve to be treated like a criminal for it. But if anyone at all gets wind that she's there, that's the story you give them. She snuck over to Kurtis to steal food and she's being detained. If anyone tries to ask questions beyond that tell them it's none of their business until she gets a fair hearing. Gromov, you're the backup location in case we need to move her for whatever reason."

"We've got a room set up for her close enough to the jail cell that we can probably pull that charade off," Renner said. "We can't keep it up forever, though. How long is this supposed to go on?"

"I don't know. Until I come up with a better plan? Or we have a complete overall idea of when and how to release this info to the public. It's been a long day. Even I can stay on my toes for only so long before I get tired. I need to rest. I need to look over the information still coming in. I need…" *I need to get laid*, she thought, but kept that to herself. "It doesn't matter what I need, I guess. What matters is what the colonies need. And the colonies need all of us to be well-rested before we make any more big decisions. Unless either of you has any more questions, that will be all."

Renner nodded and his screen went blank. Gromov took a little longer, and Westin thought she was going to say something before hers shut off as well. Westin didn't like that. Gromov was never a terribly emotional person, but Westin had seen throughout the entire conversation that she seemed to only just be keeping it together. Westin would have to keep an eye on her. She would hate to have to replace Gromov, but if she showed any further signs of resisting orders Westin might not have any choice.

"Knock knock," someone politely said at the door. Westin spun around expecting to find that someone had been spying on her for the entire conversation. Instead, it was only Metzger.

"What is it?" she asked. The words came out harsher than she had intended. Her relationship with Metzger was a strange one. He was another person that had been foisted on her by the Syndicate and there wasn't much she could do about it other than to minimize his ability to actually do anything. He was an incompetent of the first order, and Westin was sure that he'd been inflicted on her for some petty indignity Miranda Rothschild believed Westin had inflicted on her at some point in the distant past.

And yet it was hard to hate Metzger. He was a small balding man and one of the few people on the entire planet who still required glasses. According to his medical records, a family history of glaucoma prevented him from getting corrective surgery. These were the kind of things that should have prevented him from being sent to Mars in the first place if petty Syndicate politics hadn't gotten involved. Yet, despite all this and his general inability to keep up as the second-in-command of Miranda, there was no denying that he was a kind, polite, and gentle person. He always said please and thank you, he avoided interrupting anyone talking no matter how important he thought it was, and he gave everyone in the colony down to the lowest subordinate a genuine "How are you today?" whenever he saw them. And people responded with an honest answer, because he gave off that impression that he actually wanted to know.

"I'm so sorry. I hope I wasn't interrupting anything?" Metzger asked, speaking in English that was thickly colored with a German accent.

"No, I was just finished with them." She turned to look at him and saw the PDA in his hands. "Ah. I'm sorry. I forgot it was that time of day."

"No need to apologize. I was perfectly content to wait." He hit the button to turn it on before handing it to her, but he got a puzzled expression and had to hit the button again. Then again. "I… I'm sorry. I don't understand…"

How many years has this guy been here already and he still doesn't know how to turn on his PDA? Westin thought. She gestured for him to hand it to her and she took a look. She hit the power button as well but it didn't take her any more tries to understand what was wrong with it. "Did you charge it recently?"

"Oh. I suppose I didn't. My apologies."

It suddenly occurred that if "apologies" was the only word he knew in any language other than his native one then he would still be able to function the same as he already did.

"We can put it on my charger as we download your update," Westin said. "Come on."

She led him through the conference room to her office and put his PDA on the charging pad on her desk. Then she took her own from the breast pocket of her jumpsuit and configured what she would transfer. In theory, Metzger, as her second-in-command, needed all the information she had on the situation on Earth and the Bratsk virus. In truth, he didn't need much at all, but it was difficult to decide what he might actually need and what he didn't. At the very least he needed all the projection data she had for the virus's spread, since he was in charge of allocating their current resources and preserving them based how long Westin thought they might be cut off from Earth even under the best of circumstances. He didn't need anything on the supply drop, though, at least not yet. That was the kind of data that could be used to sabotage the shipment by anyone suitably psychotic enough, or even by someone like Weasel to get supplies she wasn't supposed to have. She'd give that to Metzger at a later date closer to the supply drop's landing.

She also kept all the actual messages from Miranda Rothschild to herself. Those were far too personal for anyone else, and it wasn't like there was any essential information in them that wasn't elsewhere in the data packets she gave Metzger.

After sorting out everything not to download, she connected the two PDAs with a hard line. It wouldn't take that long for the information to transfer, but there was still quite a lot of it. Just enough that she would have to sit here with Metzger for an awkward amount of time. She only hoped he wouldn't try to talk.

"And how are you doing?" Metzger asked.

Goddamn it, Westin thought. Out loud she said, "How do you think I'm doing?"

"Not well, I suppose," Metzger said. He paused before speaking again. "Do you suppose that virus can spread to animals?"

"Uh, I don't know. Why do you ask?"

"It's just that I was thinking how sad it would be. There are so many people dying. I was thinking of their pets. All those cats and dogs. No humans for them anymore. It must be so lonely for them."

Westin gaped at him. "You're joking, right?"

"No. Why would you think that?"

"Millions of humans are dying right now. Human beings. You know, people with thoughts and feelings and loved ones and hopes and dreams. And you're worried about whether or not someone is going to pet their cats?"

Metzger shrugged and looked away. "I guess I just miss having cats. And dogs too, I suppose. You know. Puppies."

Oh God, she thought. *Are those tears at the corner of his eyes? Is he about to cry?*

The PDAs beeped, indicating that the upload was complete. Westin moved perhaps a little faster than she needed to unplug Metzger's PDA and hand it back to him. That hadn't been long enough to charge it completely, but she didn't care.

"Here you go," she said. He still looked on the verge of tears. She was torn between the desperate need to get this strange little man out of her office and the desire to give him a hug. "Maybe you should go do something fun. Go to the common room. Exercise. Whatever."

"Maybe I'll do just that," he said, adding a sniff at the end. "Is there anything else you need from me right now?"

"No, just... no. Go. Er, have a good rest of the night."

"Yes, you as well. Take good care."

He finally left. Westin sat in her seat at the desk and breathed out a long sigh. It occurred to her that maybe she needed to take her own advice. She'd had stressful days running the Mars colonies before, but even the Max Perrish incident hadn't rivaled this one for sheer mental drainage. Unlike everyone else, she didn't have to go to the common room for television or entertainment, since she had everything she could want or need in her own bedroom. Well, not everything. She was just about to contact Takibana on his PDA to see if he was up for a little private time when the computer at her desk pinged that it had another v-mail message. She moved quickly to answer, sure that it would be Rochelle with another update.

Rochelle didn't appear on the screen. Kurtis Rothschild did. Westin didn't need him to explain what that meant, but he proceeded to anyway in a low monotone, that voice she had learned long ago to recognize as his way of attempting to hide his feelings.

No, Westin thought, *this can't be right. It hasn't even been a whole day since the last message. She looked fine. There wasn't anything wrong with her...*

Even as she tried to deny it to herself, Westin started to silently cry.

13

The miners could complain all they wanted about working later out on the Martian landscape as the external temperatures had dropped even further than they were used to working in, but they didn't understand what it had been like for Svensson to sit alone in his little control booth listening to them whine and sweating like a pig. The temperature controls in his control room must have been in need of repair again, or else one of the miners had come in and sabotaged them just to be petty. Either way, it was probably a low priority repair and Svensson expected it would take some time to get someone to fix it, given that Westin wanted to forgo all unnecessary maintenance until they had a better idea whether or not they would be getting future assistance from Earth. Svensson could complain all he wanted that his comfort was essential to an effective mining operation, but he doubted most people would listen.

When the miners did finally come in for the evening, the sun was low on the horizon and Svensson guessed that there wouldn't be much left in the mess hall for dinner. Barkley would have left the miners something, he assumed, while Svensson would probably be given the absolute last of the leftovers, which from personal experience he knew usually was nothing more than protein mush. There would have been something better in his own personal stores in his apartment, but Westin had confiscated most of that immediately after the meeting. None of this was fair or acceptable. As soon as things calmed back down on Earth, Svensson had every intention of logging a complaint with Kurtis Rothschild.

Svensson took a route through the corridors, narrow and few as they were, that allowed him to bypass the miners completely as they changed out of their suits and left. He didn't want to see any of them. They disgusted him. Almost every schmuck on this entire planet disgusted him. He needed to get away from them all and forget how little regard these people had for him. Maybe the best thing for all this would be to skip the dregs of dinner, instead using later what little food he'd been able to keep out of Westin's grubby paws, and just find him one of the working girls for a little dessert.

The sign-up board for the working girls was in the common room, hidden in a corner far from the television and single couch that was supposed to provide rest and entertainment to over fifty people. Svensson always hated looking at that frumpy couch. It was just one more symbol of how little importance was placed around here on personal comfort. These were the things that should have mattered when they were millions of miles from their home planet, just like the heavy wooden table in the conference room. Now that had been an example of someone who knew what they were doing. It was a pity that whoever had decorated that room hadn't been in charge of the rest of the colony.

There were two men and one woman on the couch. Svensson knew the men well enough. Nadeem Aslam and Faisal Murad were the tool and die makers, and between them and the 3-D fabrication specialist, they were responsible for creating most of the tools and parts used for the mining equipment. The woman he only knew as Something-or-Other Kapoor, whom Svensson only knew for the fact that she refused to sleep with him. The three of them were watching some Bollywood movie that looked older than all three of them combined, one of the few inane and shitty choices the people around here were given for entertainment. And yet he was sure plenty of others would be crowding in here to watch it shortly. If he had his way, he would select one of the working girls, have the message board page them that they had to do their duty, and then retreat back to his apartment where he wouldn't have to deal with these people.

The working girls' assignation board was a flat digital screen about twice the size of the average PDA that glowed blue in its solitary corner. He hadn't had any of them in particular mind when he came in, although he usually tended to avoid Weasel. He knew well enough what she did when she wasn't tending to her duty to the colony. He'd even been known to use those services from time to time, especially when word got around that she had somehow gotten her hands on e-cigs or vaping supplies. He could also only guess where she got some of her wares, and it made sense to him that most of them were probably stolen from her johns. He couldn't blame her. That was just the way whores tended to work. But he would rather not have her in his apartment where she could get her hands on things she hadn't properly earned from him.

As he got a closer look at the board, though, he saw that wouldn't be a problem anyway. Weasel had already accepted several johns for the evening and her schedule was full. The Sulford girl wasn't as full, but the board showed her with someone at the moment and it didn't look like she would be open any time soon. That left that Crick woman. Svensson could live with that. He would just continue with her tonight what he'd been doing to her early this morning.

He selected Crick from the menu and typed in his name on the keypad next to the board. She'd get a message on her PDA that he wanted her tonight and then confirm that she accepted. Usually it only took a couple seconds for any of the working girls to respond. They knew better than to keep their johns waiting, especially Svensson, given how much clout he had with the higher-ups in the Syndicate.

"Oh, hello there. I'm sorry if I'm bothering you."

Svensson turned at the sound of Metzger's voice, already dreading every single moment of interaction he would have to have with the little man. If Svensson felt Westin wasn't as good as he could be in her top position in Miranda, then Metzger's position had always come across to him as a straight up insult. In Svensson's mind, over half the population of Miranda, even Weasel or Crick, would have been a better number two than Metzger. It was a position Svensson deserved much more, yet even his connections with Kurtis Rothschild hadn't been able to override the orders of Miranda Rothschild. In the complicated triangle of power that was the three main Rothschild siblings, Miranda had somehow beaten out Kurtis in this one specific decision and there was nothing anyone else could do about it. Had it been anyone else Svensson would have been positive that he had lied and connived his way into the position of the second most powerful person in Miranda, but everyone knew Metzger wouldn't have been capable of that.

"Yes?" Svensson said. He only barely stopped himself from

saying something far more confrontational.

"Apologies," Metzger said again. "I need to get access to the assignation board, please."

"Sorry to have to tell you, Metzger, but it looks like the whores are all full for tonight. No more room."

Svensson took particular glee at the flustered expression Metzger gave at the word "whores," as though he had just insulted the man's delicate sensibilities. That glee, unfortunately, didn't last long.

"There must be some mistake," Metzger said. "I'm actually here to confirm an appointment I was already told I could make."

Svensson lapsed into swearing in his native Swedish before he realized Metzger probably didn't understand. "That's bullshit. I was just looking at it and..."

He turned to look at the board and the place where he had typed in his name. There, next to Crick's name, was the word "Denied."

"That's not right," Svensson said. Ignoring Metzger's quiet protestations, he put in his name again. This time he didn't even have to wait more than a few seconds before it told him that he was denied again.

"Excuse me, Mr. Svensson, sir, but I really do need to get to the board. I told her I would back to her shortly."

"No, you can't do that. *She* can't do that. I requested first. It's my right." Even as he said it, he stepped aside and let Metzger through. He would try it himself and find out that he'd made a mistake. If Crick had denied Svensson that could only mean that she wasn't taking on anyone at all, even if he had a serious problem with her being able to do that. She was there for his service, and he was obviously more important that Metzger. There was no way she should have been allowed to make this decision.

Yet as soon as Metzger typed in his name the word "Approved" appeared on the screen. His name then disappeared to maintain his anonymity, showing only that Crick was now booked for the evening.

"This is bullshit," Svensson said again, almost hoping that those three simple words would be enough for him to finally get his way. Metzger, though, just pushed his glasses up from where they had almost been falling off his nose and nodded to Svensson.

"Apologies. Really. I did not mean any offense. It's just that, uh, she promised me a massage."

Metzger turned and left the room as quickly as he could, likely trying his best to get out before there was any further altercation.

Svensson stood there watching him, fuming, muttering to himself that he was sick and tired of the lack of respect. It was all a conspiracy against him, he was sure of it.

Kapoor, Aslam, and Murad all sat on the couch silently until he finally left. Once he was gone, Kapoor turned to the two men and spoke to them in Punjabi. "That guy is really an asshole."

The other two just nodded in agreement.

14

Annabeth didn't usually get nervous before a trick. Most of the time there was absolutely no reason. She knew the most of the people of Miranda intimately. The majority of the men, save for the ones who had no interest in women or for one reason or another found sleeping with her distasteful, had shared a bed with her at some point as well as small number of the women. She knew what many of them liked and what they would never want to do in a million years. Even the ones that were less pleasant (yet still not so horrible that she exercised her right to bar them from her services altogether, like that Osbourne guy) were predictable. She knew as soon as she pushed that little "Approve" button on her PDA what they would want.

As far as she could tell, this time should be no different. Metzger rarely even asked for time with any of the working girls or even one of the two working boys on their visits from Rochelle and Kurtis. He rarely seemed interested in sex. On the occasions where he did, he didn't even usually want to screw. Most of the time, it was just cuddling and soft caresses with him. The one time he'd actually wanted to do it with her he'd been fumbling and clumsy yet earnest. He was a gentle man and Annabeth hated the way others always seemed to be down on him. She knew nothing about whether or not he was good at his job. She only knew that spending intimate time with him was an honest-to-God pleasant experience.

That was what made all of this harder. Leah had gone over a list with her of all the people who might have the information she needed, but Annabeth, with her more intimate knowledge of their quarters and habits, knew that most of them wouldn't work. Metzger, though, would likely have something Leah could work with. She'd already felt bad about doing this to start with, but she'd felt even worse at the idea of taking advantage of Metzger.

She'd already agreed to this, though, and following their brief planning session, Annabeth had gone out to find him and make him an offer for the evening. She found him in the workout room staring at an exercise bike as though it might want to bite him. He'd been receptive enough to her, but Annabeth couldn't help but notice that he was more distracted even than usual. She guessed that whatever was going on behind the scenes was weighing on him, and that had brought the feelings of guilt coming back to her afresh.

You're not actually doing anything wrong, she thought to herself. The plan was fairly simple, and she herself would not be doing anything she considered unethical, or at least that was what she kept telling herself. Metzger's apartment was in the administration wing, right between Svensson's and Westin's and just a few doors down from the conference room and Westin's office. Thankfully, unlike with Svensson, Metzger didn't have any bizarre problem with people seeing her coming and going from his room, although the guards that occasionally wandered the halls tended to give her dirty looks. She didn't know whether Metzger just didn't care what the other higher ups in the organization thought of him like Svensson did (a rather ridiculous taboo, Annabeth thought, considering pretty much all of them had come to her at some point or another) or if he already knew his poor reputation and didn't think there was anything that could possibly make it worse. Or maybe he was just that oblivious to what other people thought that he didn't even realize he was violating some unwritten rule by having a working girl show up outside his door. If Annabeth was forced to make a bet, she would have put it on the last one.

Once Annabeth was in, it was up to her to find Metzger's PDA and find some moment to get away from him where she could slip it just outside the door. Leah would be out in the halls somewhere doing her sneaky best to get around the guards and download what she needed from the PDA. Annabeth had asked how she would get past the password protection, causing Leah to snort. After some thought, Annabeth understood what that meant without even having to ask. Knowing Metzger, his password was probably "password."

Then, once Leah had what she needed, she would leave the PDA where she'd found it and Annabeth would be responsible for retrieving it and putting it back. All told, this should be fairly easy. Then Annabeth could get back to her honest living and would probably even be able to convince herself that she hadn't done anything wrong.

She lightly knocked on Metzger's door and waited for him to answer. Another guard passed her in the hallway with a dirty look. Annabeth did her best to ignore it, but the guard's presence disconcerted her. That was the third guard she'd seen walking through the administration wing since she'd come in. As there were only six guards in all of Miranda, including Ishikawa Takibana himself, they were usually far more spread out, and more prone to patrol the mining, production, and shipping wings as that was where the most valuable items, including the diamonds, could usually be found. The administration wing shouldn't have merited this much security. Perhaps Leah was right about something deeply disturbing going on.

Briefly, Annabeth was worried that Leah wouldn't be able to get through to find the PDA when it was left out for her. Then she remembered that this was Leah she was talking about. If Leah really wanted to get through, it would take someone or something other than a security guard to stop her.

Metzger finally opened the door and timidly peeked out at her. Some johns tried to make a grand show of letting her in. They would be dressed in something classy or tacky, usually both, which was an interesting trick considering they shouldn't have had much in the way of clothes beyond their jumpsuits. Weasel had told her once that she'd smuggled a cashmere robe onto the planet some time back. Annabeth had countered that she must have gotten more than just one, considering how many men were wearing one when they let her in. Weasel had laughed and said that no, she'd only managed to get one to Mars, and no one other than her would have been able to do it. Following that, Annabeth had kept a close eye on the robes, noting the way that each and every one happened to be worn or threadbare in the same spot. She even noted a small, stiff stain that she'd accidently left on the robe with one client had still been there with the next. Apparently, whoever kept trading or selling the stupid thing to the next person trying to impress her never bothered to get it clean. Finally,

Annabeth had offered to pay for the chemical cleaning herself and "misplaced" it before she got that far. Oops.

Metzger, however, had never put on that kind of air in the past and he didn't now. When he opened the door, he was still in his jumpsuit with the zipper pulled down halfway. He wore a thin undershirt that did little to hide the darkness of his hairy chest. "Annabeth," he said, then looked down as though he had said something he should be ashamed of. "Miss Crick."

"Annabeth's fine," she said. If she recalled correctly, this was the same exact exchange they'd had on the few others times they'd gotten together. Metzger was nothing if not a creature of habit. "May I come in…" She paused, trying to make it sound like a sexy come on. In truth, it took her a couple extra seconds to remember his first name. "…Hans?"

"Yes, of course," he said. He stepped aside and waved her in like a butler letting in an important guest. Annabeth, strangely inspired by the gesture, responded with a short curtsy. His face lit up and Annabeth was reminded why she liked her rare appointments with him. Many of her johns felt like they had a right to her time. Metzger, on the other hand, appreciated every moment of it.

The interior of his apartment was, structurally, an exact replica of the one she had left Svensson in this morning. It had the little kitchenette on one side near the door and an emergency airlock on the other with the bed and living space between. That was where the similarities ended, though, as Metzger's was meticulously clean compared to the disgusting sty Svensson allowed himself to live in. Not that she could complain about that given the way she herself lived. It was just a reminder that she was not at all in the same position she was usually in.

And I'm about to take advantage of it in the worst way, she thought, although she quickly forced that thought away.

"May I offer you something to…" he started to say as he opened his small refrigerator, but before she could see what he had inside to offer he shut it and blushed. "Uh, apologies. I don't have anything anymore. I completely forgot."

Curious, she thought. As Miranda's second-in-command, there was no reason he should have been short of anything he wanted. If

Svensson could tempt her into overtime with an egg then Metzger should have been able to do much more. She heard Leah's niggling voice in her head saying yet again that something strange was going on, but she ignored it.

"Don't worry," Annabeth said. "I just had dinner anyway. Barkley's noodles were… interesting, as always."

He laughed, a noise that he immediately seemed to be self conscious about. "Yes, so… I was wondering why you specifically made an offer to me today. If I may ask."

She looked at his breast pocket and the PDA sticking out that it would probably fall out, likely unnoticed by him, if he bent over. "What, you don't think I occasionally like to see you?"

"No. I know what people think of me. Usually I'm okay with it. I can accept it. Although sometimes I—"

"Get lonely?" Annabeth asked.

"Yes."

"Then maybe that's why I'm here."

"Is it really?"

"Does it matter?"

He gave her a wan smile and then gestured toward his bed. "No, I guess not."

Annabeth smiled back at him, then proceeded to unzip her jumpsuit.

15

I swore I wouldn't do this again, Leah thought to herself. *No more hacking. No more breaking into anyone else's property. This isn't supposed to be me anymore. I left that part of me behind.*

As she moved through the halls of Miranda, doing her best to avoid anyone who might remember her skulking around where she shouldn't, she had to wonder how true that was. The need to know what others said she shouldn't was grown deep inside her. She didn't want to compare it to her gender, since that was such a deeply rooted part of her identity that nothing else could truly compare, but it did feel like another part of the complex tapestry her life had woven, showing a repeated picture of trying to deny what she was and then coming back to it.

This time is different, she thought. *I'm not trying to find out what's going on for myself. I'm doing it for Dip and Weasel and Kleinstock...*

She sighed. But mostly she was doing it for herself. Fine. The sooner she admitted that, the sooner she could actually enjoy the hunt.

Before she had even gotten as far as the administration wing, she noted the lack of guards in most of their usual places. She'd taken a path that went near the gem storage room and saw the typical guard there, although that was usually redundant given the other security measures rumored to be in place beyond its door. She'd memorized the typical patrol patterns of the other guards long ago, and she should have seen more on her way here. That only led her to believe they were looking out for something out of the ordinary, and it wouldn't surprise her if that was in the administration wing, right where she wanted to be.

She confirmed this when she crossed the threshold into the wing. She heard two guards whispering quietly to each other and backed out the door back in the common wing, keeping out of general sight until they were gone. She knew the voices, Monique Kristfal and Aishwarya Simmons, although she didn't know much about them beyond the fact that Simmons was Deputy Chief of Security, second behind Takibana. Leah didn't usually feel a need to get to know anyone even remotely involved with the security force. She had far too many bad memories of the police back on Earth.

On a hunch she didn't move, staying where she was until she heard footsteps again. They weren't talking this time, but the light sound of their steps seemed to suggest it was the same people. So they were on a regular circuit. Good, that would be easy enough to avoid.

When they were gone again, she stepped back in the administration wing. The office where she had her own cubicle would be down to the right, where the two guards had gone. From there the wing formed a large, squared figure eight. The security station and Miranda's handful of jail cells, rarely used, where further down on the far side of the eight from her. The administrators' quarters and offices would be to her left. She started to go that way then thought better of it, realizing that she would eventually run into the guards as they came back around. Instead, she followed their path, although being sure to keep enough of a gap between them that they wouldn't hear her.

She went past her work area and stopped just before the crossbar of the eight. If she were seen where she was standing now, she could pass it off as her just heading to her cubicle to get some extra work done, but beyond this point it would look highly suspect if anyone saw her skulking around. Under normal circumstances, nothing about this area was off limited, but she could hear additional voices at the security station and down the crossbar. There were a few rest rooms down there along with Metzger and Anguitine's offices, nothing worth guarding as far as Leah knew. Leah took a quick look down that hall and saw another guard, Matsumoto Haruma, standing just outside Anguitine's office and speaking to her inside in Japanese. Leah didn't speak that one so she wasn't sure what they were saying, but Matsumoto had a vaguely flirty way of leaning against the doorway. Leah supposed maybe he wasn't on duty, but his presence just made her more on edge. He wasn't looking this direction, though, so Leah slipped past the hall and on down past the security station. She still heard the voices there but no one was in any position to see her slink away.

I'm really not liking this, she thought to herself, although her body responses seemed to tell a different story. The way her heart fluttered could have just been nervousness at getting caught, but there was feeling in her stomach as well, that kind of butterfly feeling people were supposed to get when they were infatuated. She recognized that as the thrill of once again not doing what she'd been told. It was the question, charging her onward, of whether or not she could get away with something.

The walls here, like everywhere, were thick and insulated to protect against a catastrophic loss of pressure, but as she came around the far side of the eight she thought she heard something rhythmic coming from behind the walls. At first she didn't think anything of it, except the closer she got the more organic it sounded, like it was accompanied by heavy breathing or voices. She paused, her curiosity getting the better of her desire to keep moving, and listened more intently. After a few seconds, she finally understood what she was hearing.

Ah, Annabeth, you little vixen, Leah thought. *So much for Metzger only wanting a massage.* Except when she thought about it, that couldn't be right either. Metzger's apartment wouldn't be until around the next corner and down a little farther, between Westin's apartment and Svensson's. As for where she was now, there was only the conference room and Westin's office...

The office door, she realized, was closed. She leaned in closer and listened. That wasn't Annabeth at all. That was Westin breathing and groaning. Someone else too, although Leah couldn't be sure. Probably Takibana.

She stepped away from the door, fighting to keep a smile from her face. She certainly couldn't blame anyone for scratching an itch, although she had to admit she was jealous. When her and Martin were getting busy, she had to either do it in her room, where Annabeth may or may be depending on whether or not she was on a job (not that Annabeth minded) or they had to do it in his apartment which he shared with Schwartzmann the meteorologist (who most definitely *did* mind). It had to be nice to not only have a private place to do it, but also to have two different options. Unless

Takibana's place would also work, but it was over in the same wing as Leah's, past the common wing and closer to mining and shipping.

None of that was her business, of course, and had nothing to do with the task at hand. She was only concerned about one couple being intimate in this wing. Leah looked around the next corner to see it empty. There were six doors here, four on the outer side and two on the inner. For now, Leah was only concerned with the second down on the outer side. That was Metzger's. It also didn't have a PDA sitting just outside of it yet.

Leah pulled herself back around the corner and thought for a second. She hadn't expected it would be out here immediately, but she also hadn't quite anticipated the number of guards. She might be able to do one or two laps around the wing without being noticed, but do it too much and everyone would start to get suspicious. She also couldn't stay here, not with the guards still walking their circuit, and she couldn't just leave. Even for someone as notoriously absent-minded as Metzger, it would be a noticeable sight to see a PDA just sitting out in the cramped hallway. Someone would notice it and grab it if it were out here for too long.

Leah started to consider where there might be a room or door she could hide behind until Annabeth was ready, but before she could come up with any decent ideas she heard a voice calling her name.

"Hartnup? What are you doing here?"

She silently cursed herself. The voice had come from further down Metzger's hall. The owner must have seen her poke her head out, or else she perhaps wasn't hiding as well as she'd thought. She took a deep breath, preparing for it to be one of the guards, and stepped out into view.

It wasn't a guard though. She'd still been certain she would be able to talk her way around a guard if she needed. She hadn't been prepared, however, to have to talk to Svensson.

16

Mars still had gravity, of course. If you fell down, it still hurt. But in a gravity that was thirty-eight percent that of Earth, it was low enough that it changed the way a person had to interact with her environment. Most of these changes Westin barely noticed anymore. The one she had never gotten over, however, the one that still both delighted and confounded her to this day, was the way Mars' gravity affected sex. It was easy to get carried away when every tiny body movement, especially those that caused a person to bounce up and down, could send you right up off the bed or furniture before bringing you back down in an oddly pillowed fashion. And she'd gotten even more carried away this time than usual. They had accidentally knocked a few things off her desk that had come raining down like a slow motion hailstorm, and they'd nearly upended the chair they'd been on. Now that Westin and Takibana were done, the office would look to the casual observer like they'd just had a wild and passionate romp only suitable to be seen in a porno.

However, that hadn't at all been what it felt like for Westin. There had been no joy in it for her, and Takibana had been strangely grim as well. Their quickie hadn't been a fun, joyous celebration of life. It had been more of a comfort screw, a confirmation that they were still alive and capable of continuing on with life. Westin had to wonder now, though, how long that would last.

When she'd asked Takibana to come by, she hadn't needed to tell him why, and he hadn't asked. Westin supposed that her tone of voice and the tears she was fighting to hold back were enough to let him know what the latest v-mail from Earth had said. Maybe the last v-mail, for all she knew.

Now, as she stepped away from Takibana, still sitting limp and exhausted in her desk chair with his jumpsuit around his ankles, she realized she had nothing else with which to keep the abject fear at bay. The entire day had been shocking. She wasn't even sure how so much terrible news could fit into a twenty-five hour period in the first place. When she'd woken up this morning, she'd only had the barest clues of what was happening back on Earth. And it had all gone so wrong so unbelievably fast.

Kurtis had confirmed her worst fears in the v-mail as soon as he had started speaking. Rochelle had started showing symptoms soon after she'd sent the last v-mail. She was now confined, but he said she was coughing up blood now at an alarming rate. For once, he had actually seemed concerned for one of his siblings, which Westin knew from experience was a sign of just how bad things were. He had even looked pale and sweaty as he spoke, and his voice had gone from his normal abrupt way of speaking to a slight slur. He hadn't mentioned the state of Miranda or any of his other siblings, but Westin already had her guesses.

Beyond the dire fate of the Rothschild's themselves, Kurtis spoke long enough to make Westin sure the people of Mars would not be getting any more help from anyone else on Earth, either. The spread of the Bratsk virus was already quicker than anybody had anticipated. Most of Europe and parts of the United States were known to be exposed. He said it was getting harder to be certain of the factuality of the information he had, since the news reports from around the globe were getting more and more chaotic. All contact with Russian officials had been cut off. There was talk of riots in pretty much every country throughout the whole world, and lots of unconfirmed reports of entire hospitals being ransacked for supplies. The one detail that Westin had latched onto, though, and one of the few that Kurtis could confirm with absolute certainty, was the destruction of the Rothschilds' primary launch sites in Florida and Switzerland. The India site had been spared, but considering that one had just been used only a day earlier for the latest supply rocket, there wasn't much chance of it being used again so quickly. Both sites had been destroyed at approximately the same time, so the obvious implication was terrorism, but in all the mess no one yet had any clue who was responsible, and multiple conflicting groups had claimed responsibility. So the Syndicate didn't know yet the precise reason why they had been targeted, yet the consequences were clear. There would be no more supplies sent from Earth. The shuttle launched earlier would be the last one. Kurtis said that if things eventually calmed down they would be able to figure something out as far as future supplies.

If. Westin had watched that section of the v-mail several times to make sure that was the word she had heard. Kurtis was not the kind to use that word. Usually he would have said "when." The presence of "if," as far as Westin was concerned, was the ultimate confirmation.

The Bratsk virus had annihilated the Mars colonies' support system back on Earth. That would be no help. There would be no going back. If they were lucky, Westin would receive a few more messages before Earth went completely dark, but even Kurtis' email had cut off abruptly, exactly like she'd had Kleinstock do to Dip Benegal's message this morning. Except this one hadn't been cut off artificially.

Okay, so I know what has happened and what is truly at stake now, Westin thought. *The lives of 155 other people. For all I know, the last people. Once the virus is done, the population of Mars might just be all that's left of the human race.*

Westin found her bra where it had been thrown under her desk and considered that thought. She didn't know for sure that was the case. There might have been people on Earth who were immune, or the death rate might have been somewhat exaggerated. There would almost definitely be small enclaves of paranoid preppers who had decided the end was upon them and locked themselves away. So no, the colonies probably wouldn't be the last of the human race in reality. But for their purposes, it might as well be true.

And the death of billions of people on their home world will cause a panic here. No doubt, Westin thought. There couldn't be any more hiding this. She'd been telling herself she was doing it for everyone's own good with the idea that it would blow over, but that wouldn't work anymore. The first thing she needed to do, after she got dressed again, was formulate how she would accomplish such a thing without causing riots.

"You're going to need to gather up all your stun guns in one place," Westin said. She grabbed her underwear from where it had ended up on the corner of her desk yet stared at it for a second before she put it on. It was strange how the mind worked in a crisis. Here she was, trying to think of what she needed to do next to keep her people alive on a planet where nothing should be able to live, and the first thing that was occurring to her now was that they'd run out of sanitary pads soon. That would actually be a major problem, since exactly fifty-one percent of Mars' current population were women. And toilet paper. What little fibrous plants they had growing in Kurtis wouldn't be enough to convert into things like that. All of this was a problem that needed to be solved, but later rather than sooner.

"Not your usual after-the-act kind of talk," Takibana said.

"This is not time for joking," Westin said. "Back to being professional."

"Okay, fine then," Takibana said. "We already have all the stun guns together in the security station. You know that."

"I do know that, just as I know that's not going to be enough. Everyone in Miranda knows that location. I want them in a location that only you and a few trusted people in your staff know about."

"You think someone's going to steal them? No one would do that."

"No one would do that now," Westin said. "But after they know humanity is now just more or less us? Who knows who will act like what?"

"Don't you think you're exaggerating?"

"Excuse me?"

"I know it's bad on Earth, but it's not like the population is going to get wiped out. That's just not how these things work."

Westin made a noncommittal grunt as she stepped into the legs of her jumpsuit. She stared at Takibana and the way he still sat half-naked in the chair, suddenly realizing that she was seeing the other half of the colonies' inevitable reaction. A large number would panic, yes. Others, though, would be in denial. Ishikawa here had grown up in Kyoto, born a number of years after the Fukushima incident. Neither he nor any of his family had been living in Japan anymore by the time of the devastating Nagoya earthquake, having relocated to Australia where his father was a shipping manager for the Rothschild Syndicate's opal concerns there. That family had died long ago, although not in any single great tragedy. His father had died of colon cancer, his mother from a heart attack. Westin didn't know anything about the whereabouts of his brother, although from his lack of concern she suspected that either he had died too or they were so estranged that Ishikawa wouldn't shed a tear at the thought of his death.

He had, in short, never been up close and personal with a full scale disaster. They were things he saw on the news that didn't affect him in anything more than an ephemeral way. There would be others like him, although how many Westin couldn't say. It wasn't that they wouldn't care, it was that they would lack the context to understand the true horror of the situation.

"How much do you trust me?" Westin asked.

"Do you even need to ask that?"

"Just humor me. Please."

"I trust you absolutely."

"And even if you didn't trust me, what would that mean?" Westin already knew the answer, but she needed to see that his reaction would match his inevitable words. She wasn't disappointed. She was sure he didn't do it purposefully, but he immediately sat up straighter in his chair and took on an air of dignity, which was an interesting feat considering his current clothing situation.

"I would still follow your orders."

Westin nodded. That was what had attracted her to him in the first place. He was a man who could always be trusted to put duty before his emotions. It was the only reason Westin hadn't felt more than the minimal ethical quandary in having a sexual relationship with him. They both enjoyed each other's company, maybe even cared for each other, but they also understood that if they were forced with the decision between each other or the colonies, the colonies came first. Always.

"Then here are my orders. Take this fucking seriously. I've only told you a small portion of what I know, and I'll be doling out everything else I know to everyone in easily digestible chunks. Not all at once, I think. As far as everyone else on the planet knows, we'll be getting our first indication that something is wrong on Earth tomorrow. It'll be a long process. We'll let the three colony psychologists know what's really going on and have them keep a close eye on reactions. But you and the security staff will need to be ready in case something goes wrong. Do I make that clear?"

"You do," Takibana said. He stood up to pull up his underwear and jumpsuit, although he paused before he zipped it. "So this is really happening? You honestly believe the cutoff from Earth is permanent?"

Westin paused to make sure that she herself was sure before she answered. "Yes."

"You're not acting like it," he said. "I know you hold yourself together really well, but this…"

"What we just did is about the extent of my emotional reaction," Westin said.

"But didn't you say you had loved ones back home? I'd have at least thought I'd see you cry."

Westin thought back to what Kurtis had said about Rochelle. "You're not going to see that. As much as I may trust you, you'll never see that. Understood?"

He went over to her and kissed her on the cheek, the closest either of them ever allowed a show of affection outside of sex. "Crystal," he said.

That was about the time Westin finally heard the raised voices out in the hall.

17

"Svensson," Leah said. She rarely had interactions with him, but the ones she did were usually not pleasant. While he tended to talk politely enough in public, everyone knew the stories the miners would tell about his generally shitty attitude, as well as all the stories Annabeth had told her about his way of acting in the bedroom. She supposed it made sense that he would be here, considering his apartment was only one door down. He was an annoyance, but Leah doubted he would be any problem once she managed to get rid of him. The question was how.

"You're not supposed to be here, are you?" Svensson asked.

Leah did her best to act indignant. "I work in this wing. I can be here as much as I want."

His eyes narrowed. "You work all the way on the other side of the wing. Not here. This is where we live." Leah caught the implied meaning there. This was where important people lived. Anyone that didn't meet Svensson's standards shouldn't be seen near them. It was the same attitude that resulted in him forcing Annabeth to walk to and from his apartment through the frozen Martian desert.

"Is there a problem here?" someone asked from behind Leah. She turned and had to force herself not to curse out loud. Simmons and Kristfal had come back around in their circuit. Both of them had their stun guns out and in the open rather than in their holsters, as though they had already been told to expect to use them.

On Earth, she would have run. Here there was nowhere to go. On this entire planet, there were only a few square kilometers of buildings with breathable air, and just under two thirds of them somewhere else out across the wastes. The only option she had now was to try to talk her way out, or else end up in a jail cell after admitting she was trying to steal secret information from the deputy director.

Before she could say anything, Svensson answered for her. "There's no problem. I just asked Hartnup here to talk about some software updates in my control booth."

Neither of the guards questioned that. They simply continued on down the hall and vanished again around the corner.

"Why would you say that?" Leah whispered, mindful of the possibility that someone else might walk around the corner and hear her.

"You're up to no good, aren't you?" Svensson asked. "Not that I suppose you'll tell me. No one ever tells me. But I always know."

"If you really think that then why would you cover for me?"

"You're roommates with Crick. You must have drawn the short straw, rooming with a whore. Do you know why she refused me today to fuck Metzger instead?"

Oh Jesus, is that really what this is about? Leah thought. "No, I don't have any idea."

"Don't lie to me. I'm smarter than that. I know you two spend a lot of time together. I know she would have told you."

Leah had been getting closer to him this whole time, and now she found herself just outside Metzger's door. She would probably be able to lean her ear against it and get some idea of how far along Annabeth and Metzger were, just like she had outside Westin's office. For all she knew, Annabeth could have been on the other side, waiting for their voices to go away so that she could place the PDA where Leah could get it. But nothing was going to happen as long as Svensson stood here.

"Maybe she just wanted someone a little different today," Leah said. What she really wanted to say was that maybe Annabeth had wanted to work with someone for a change who wasn't a complete prick. Somehow she didn't think that would be very productive.

"It doesn't matter what she wanted. I put in an order first. I have a right to her, not him."

"Wait, excuse me? She's a human being. You don't have a right at all. She gets to choose."

"She's a whore, and she has to do what the Syndicate says. And if the Syndicate says she has to fuck me, then she does."

Holy Christ, what the hell has gotten into him today? Leah thought. She'd always known he wasn't a nice guy, but this was beyond any of his usual behavior. It was like every single person in charge around here had taken crazy pills bright and early this morning and everyone under them had to deal with the inexplicable consequences.

"That's not how her job works and you know it," Leah said. She wondered if he had somehow managed to get drunk, but alcohol was a substance so banned on Mars that even Weasel didn't deal in it. Or maybe someone had managed to set up some kind of moonshine still and Svensson had gotten into it. *Or maybe the stress of whatever's going down is turning him into the greatest asshole on the entire planet*, she thought.

"You can either tell me why she refused me, or I can find the next security guards and report you for skulking," he said.

"Skulking? There's officially a rule against that now? In a wing where I'm allowed anyway?" She hoped she sounded sufficiently sure of herself, even though she was sure that "skulking" in the current situation (whatever the hell that even was) would still be at least enough to put her in a cell for the next day or two. It suddenly occurred to her that after five years on the planet keeping her nose clean, that simple infraction might be enough to violate her contract with the Syndicate and result in the forfeiture of all the money she'd earned. If she were charged with breaking the Syndicate's version of laws, she would return to Earth in even worse shape than when she'd started.

I should have just let all this go, she thought.

No, screw that shit, she thought the next moment. *I need to know what's going on. And I'm willing to bet my money and my freedom that everyone else in Miranda needs to know as well.*

"Excuse me, just what is going on out here?" someone said from behind Leah again. This time she knew who it was just by the sound of her voice. Leah turned to see Westin coming down the hall from her office, her jumpsuit still unzipped just enough for Leah to see that she wasn't wearing an undershirt. Svensson turned beat red.

"Nothing," he said. "Nothing's going on."

"Didn't sound like nothing." Westin looked at Leah and raised an eyebrow. "What are you doing here?"

"I was just asking the same thing," Svensson said.

"And you were asking it in a very loud and disturbing manner,"

Westin said. She turned back to Leah again. "So what is the answer?"

"Nothing," Leah said, although she knew that would hardly be enough to get them to leave her alone. "Nothing at all. I was just…" She looked at Metzger's door again. "I got done doing some extra work and I knew Annabeth was doing a job with Metzger. I just thought I'd see if she was done before I went back."

Westin looked at Svensson. "And you? For some reason you don't seem very happy about that."

Leah could see the effort it took for him to keep from shouting. "I have business with Crick as well."

"Then I don't see how that involves Hartnup here. Why don't you let her go about her business, then?"

"Westin, ma'am, something is not right here. Hartnup and Crick are up to something."

"Svensson, I know you see people plotting against you everywhere you go," Westin said, "but sometimes they're really not. Most of the time, in fact."

"Is that the kind of security risk you really want to take? Given what… uh…" Svensson didn't finish his sentence, but it didn't look like he needed to. Leah had thought for a moment there that she would walk away from this without any further problem, but whatever Svensson was talking about Westin immediately took his meaning. Her demeanor changed from vaguely annoyed to icy.

"Go back to your apartment," Westin said to him.

"But…"

"Do it. I'll investigate here."

"But Crick…"

"Is no more of your concern right now. Go away or I'll slap you with a few days in a jail cell for insubordination."

Svensson stepped back like he had been smacked, an expression of pure confusion on his face. It didn't last for long though. Just before he turned around to go back to his apartment, Leah thought she saw a hint of bitter rage coming to the surface. She made a note to tell Annabeth that she might want to avoid him for a few days. Even though he had never been violent before, Leah thought he might do things he normally wouldn't to Annabeth if he got her alone in this mood.

Once Svensson had shut his door, Westin turned all of her attention back to Leah. "So are you up to something?"

"No! I'm just…"

"The last time anyone saw you at your cubicle was hours ago. I've been having security keep an eye on every coming and going. You did not just finish with your work."

Leah almost said something but decided at the last second to keep her mouth shut. Nothing she could say would get her out of this now, so the best thing she could do was keep from incriminating herself. At the same time, she was surprised. Westin had just admitted that security was higher. In Leah's mind, that was confirmation that everything was out of whack.

"Hartnup, I don't know if we've ever really talked," Westin said. "I get the impression that you don't like me, but based on your psych eval I'm betting that has more to do with your issues with authority than any specific grievance with me. Would that be correct?"

Leah still didn't say anything but she was sure she didn't have to. Westin knew full well that she was right.

"So I'm going to make a guess," Westin continued. "You know something is going on. I'm betting you've even tried to use some of your computer skills to find out what it is. I'm going to do you a favor and respect your intelligence by not lying to you. But you know very well why we sensor certain information from Earth. We are on a world that wants to kill us. We won't survive unless things are done cautiously and with every eventuality covered. That's always the way it has been since the beginning. So I'm asking you to do this: please let this go for now. Everyone will understand eventually. Even if you don't like the way I'm doing things, only realize that I'm doing them this way to keep people alive."

Westin stopped and stared at Leah. Leah could only assume that she thought this would be enough time for Leah to absorb what she was saying. Leah had to admit it was hard to disagree at the moment. Westin had charisma and strength and she was someone that you wanted to believe knew what she was doing. For just a moment, Leah almost wanted to do as she said.

Except Leah couldn't do that. It was hardwired into her head to not trust the popular and charismatic ones, had been since childhood when it was exactly those kinds of people who had organized others to gang up on her all because she'd acted too feminine for their liking. Now that she knew for certain, confirmed by Westin herself, that something big was happening, she knew she would have no choice but to keep digging. It was who she was, and she refused to deny her true nature.

But Westin didn't need to know that just yet. Instead, Leah did her best to look like she was considering it, although she knew better than to say anything. Westin was smart. All it would take was one wrong word and Leah would clue her in to the fact that she wasn't planning on playing along.

As it was, Leah couldn't be sure that Westin believed she would cooperate or not. After a few more seconds of pausing Westin pointed at Metzger's door. "So are you going to check to see if she's done or not?"

"Oh no, I don't want to disturb..."

"You said just a minute ago that you were. Suddenly changed your mind?" After another moment of hesitation Westin asked, "Or is there something more you're not telling me?"

"No, not at all."

"Then I'm sure no one at all will mind if I just check in with Metzger, will they? If nothing is out of the ordinary, we can just apologize for disturbing them and let them continue on with their business, right?"

Westin knocked on the door before Leah could say anything, not that she thought there would be anything to hide. It wasn't like Annabeth had gone in there with the intent on murdering him or anything. There wouldn't be anything incriminating behind that door.

Or at least Leah thought there wouldn't. Now that the thought had occurred to her, she was suddenly convinced that as soon as Westin opened that door, she would see Annabeth in a compromising position that had absolutely nothing to do with sex.

Both Leah and Westin were shocked when the door almost immediately opened from the other side to show Metzger, his jumpsuit on but unzipped, staring at them with even more bewilderment than was normal for him.

"Um, may I help you?" he asked.

"Is Crick in there with you?" Westin asked.

"I'm afraid I don't understand any of what is going on," Metzger said.

"Is she in there or not?" Westin asked.

Metzger stepped aside, showing Leah the answer. Other than crumpled bed sheets, there was no sign that Annabeth had even been there.

18

True to the norm, Metzger wanted very little from Annabeth. Both of them stripped naked and Metzger got on the bed face down, his arms cushioning his head while Annabeth straddled his legs. She took the one vaguely sexual thing she had ever seen in Metzger's possession, a tube of oil, and squirted a small amount on her hands.

"Hans, are you sure you don't want more than the usual?" she asked.

"No, thank you Annabeth. I would not feel comfortable."

"It would be perfectly okay if that's what you wanted," Annabeth said. "That's why I'm here." She applied the oil to his back, hairy as it was in some places, and gently kneaded it into his muscles.

"May I ask you a personal question?" he asked.

"Sure, as long as you know I reserve the right to not answer it."

"Don't you want to escape this life?"

"What's there to escape? I chose this."

"You did, so you keep saying, as does Jeanette Weasel. But there are rumors that Karen Sulford did not."

Annabeth had heard these rumors herself, but she didn't know how to answer. Karen was always quiet about how and why she had ended up as another working girl on Mars. When she'd first come here, she'd only just reached the age of majority, or so Annabeth had been told. Truthfully, it wasn't like there would have been any laws against it on this planet if she were underage. Annabeth wanted to think that such a thing couldn't happen, that everyone in this line of work on Mars was doing it because he or she had chosen it, but the only person who knew for sure was Karen, and she would only speak to Weasel about her life before this. There was no way to be sure, and no way to ease any questions in Annabeth's mind about it.

"Don't be silly," Annabeth said.

"I am just not comfortable with the possibility. So no, this is fine for me."

"You're the client," she said. She looked over at the pile of clothes they had left on the floor. His PDA was half out of the breast pocket, easy enough for her to grab now if she could only get away from him for a minute or two. She just didn't have any idea how she would justify interrupting their session and taking the PDA to the door without him seeing.

Or I could just not do it at all, she thought. *That would be the right thing to do here. Whatever the hell Leah thinks is on there, if it gets out it could come back to him.* And she didn't want that. It was more than just a question of professional ethics and courtesy. She genuinely liked Metzger. No, he wasn't the kind she would have slept with if she wasn't getting paid, but then he wasn't sleeping with her anyway. And part of that apparently was that he had a conscience about what they were doing, however misplaced it might be. That wasn't something she would have heard from most of her other clients, even the occasional woman.

Metzger made a noise like Annabeth had just hit a particularly sensitive spot on his back, although he wasn't particularly indicative of whether or not that had been a bad thing. She was just about to ask him when she heard the voices just outside his door.

Immediately, she pounced on the opportunity. "What's that?" she asked.

"Someone in the hallway? I'm sure it doesn't concern us."

"Just a second. Let me check anyway."

Most of her other clients would have complained. Metzger just moved his head a little in his arms in what she assumed was a nod of consent.

Annabeth got off him and went to the pile of clothes as though she were looking for something to cover herself up. She glanced back at him just long enough to confirm that his head was still down before she took the PDA and hid it in her bra and underwear, which she then grabbed and acted like she was going to put them on.

She had expected the voices to be nothing more that people passing by in the hall, but as she got closer Annabeth realized there were two people arguing right outside the door, and neither of them sounded like they were going to be walking away any time soon. She almost opened the door just enough to see who it was, except by the time she had reached it the two voices were loud enough that she could identify who it was even through the thick polymer that made up the door. Leah's voice wasn't surprising while Svensson's was. Even with raised voices, though, she couldn't quite be certain what they were saying. Whatever it was, it wasn't good.

Holy shit, did she just get caught? Annabeth thought. Maybe. That left her to wonder what, if anything, she should do now. If that was what was happening, then obviously Leah's plan was over. Annabeth felt relieved for a moment that she was off the hook, although that was followed immediately by shame that she would put herself ahead of her friend. And there was the other problem, the fact that Leah had honestly believed something important was on this PDA that needed to be let out into the open. If Leah was right, that meant Annabeth would be responsible for whatever bad things might happen without that information.

Make a decision, she thought to herself. *One way or the other*.

It wasn't hard. One option required her to remain faithful to a code of conduct that she believed in deeply. But the other required her to be faithful to the woman who had become like a sister to her. Once she thought of it that way, the choice was obvious.

She listened beside the door for a few more seconds, just enough to make her think this wasn't going to resolve itself quickly. She heard another voice, one she couldn't recognize, but that was just enough to make her think that the situation had gone completely out of control.

Annabeth whirled around and looked at Metzger. He still hadn't looked up, which was a good thing because she realized she still had his PDA sticking out of the pile of undergarments in her hands. Before he could look up, she went for her jumpsuit and started putting it on with a speed she had learned from many a time of being told to get out of someone's place before someone else realized she'd been there. The PDA slipped into one of her sleeves where it left a tell-tale bulge, but only if she allowed Metzger to see her from the right angle. Adjusting herself so he couldn't, she said, "I need your environment suit. Right away."

"Huh?" he said, finally looking up.

"I've got to leave and I can't go through the halls. It's an emergency." Before he could even give his consent, she was taking his suit from its alcove near the airlock. She wasn't one hundred percent sure what she thought she would accomplish here other than getting the PDA to a safe location before Metzger realized it was gone. He would, after all, miss it soon enough and probably know who had taken it. Then again, maybe not, given his reputation for being scatter-brained. Perhaps she'd be able to get it back to their apartment and hide it before anyone realized something strange was going on, although if Leah was caught, she didn't know if Leah would be in any position to do anything with it. Either way, Annabeth had to at least try, and if she couldn't go out through the hallway there was only one other option.

"But... I don't understand," Metzger said. "What is so important?"

"It's just... uh..." She didn't know how to end the sentence so she didn't try. She just stepped into the boots on the environment suit and pulled it together.

"That won't... uh, I don't think it will fit you," Metzger said. Even as he said it, Annabeth realized that would be a problem. She was hardly tall, but Metzger was short by anyone's standards, and also proportioned quite differently around the chest and stomach. It was decidedly uncomfortable even before she tried to get the helmet on, and that only made it worse as the helmet pushed uncomfortably down on her crown once she latched it. Even in her hurry, she thought enough to give it a quick once over for rips or cracks, discovering quickly that she didn't need to worry. This wasn't one of the outdated Russian suits like she was usually forced to wear. Metzger, despite probably never having to use it, was given a much newer model.

"Wait," Metzger said as he stumbled out of bed to snatch up his own clothes.

"I can't, I have to go," Annabeth said as she hit the button to open the inner door of the airlock.

"But you forgot something!" Metzger said, holding up something he'd picked up off the floor. She was both amused and annoyed to realize that at some point she'd dropped her underwear and forgotten to put it on yet again.

"You can keep it," she said, then stepped through the door and closed it behind her. Just before the air cycled out, Annabeth thought she could hear someone knocking on Metzger's door, but she didn't turn around to see who it was through the window. Instead, she opened up the outer door and found herself back on Mars' hellish tundra.

19

Svensson would have slammed the door of his apartment behind him if the doors hadn't all been designed with pneumatic cushioning to keep people from doing damage with just that kind of action. This was all just too much. No one gave him the respect he deserved, not even that bitch Westin. Always plotting, always talking down to him. They were all against him, yet there was nothing he could do to teach any of them respect. He could take it from Westin, he could even bite the bullet with Hartnup. But the one that got to him was Crick. She was nothing but a whore. She had no right to treat him like this. Him, a hand-picked appointee to the colony by Kurtis Rothschild himself.

There were any number of things Svensson could have done then. He could have left his apartment and stormed off to take his anger out on some other subordinate. He could have gone to his bed and tried to sleep it off. Even if he had started pacing at that point, every single event that came afterward would have been different. He did none of those things. Instead, he walked over to the wall next to the airlock and slammed his palm repeatedly against the wall in outrage.

Something had to be done. Anything. He couldn't let this stand, and his rage had hit a point where logic no longer would have swayed him away.

His position next to the airlock gave him a perfect view when he looked up and out the window. The windows through the two airlock doors were positioned so that he didn't have very good view of anything other than the land directly in front of it, a large portion of open, mostly level ground before the rock pushed up a kilometer in the distance to form the outer rim of Poynting Crater. But he thought he saw movement, which was so rare on the surface when there wasn't a storm that he took note. At first all he saw was a shadow, then a form lumbered into view, moving with as much speed as the unwieldy environment suits would allow.

The angle of the two windows only allowed him a view of the

person for less than a second, but that was enough. There was no way to see the person's face through the visor from here, but there weren't a lot of places the person could have come from. In that direction, there was only Westin and Metzger's airlocks, and it couldn't be Westin. She wouldn't have had time to get back to her room and into her suit following his run-in with her in the hallway. That left Metzger, but the brief glimpse he'd had suggested it wasn't him, either. It was his suit, perhaps, but it bulged in all the wrong places: not enough in the stomach and too much in the chest.

And, covered in an environment suit or not, Svensson would recognize that chest anywhere.

Crick.

To Svensson's mind, it was a long, well-thought out decision. In truth, it only took him three seconds to reach for his own environment suit. He didn't even know what he intended to do, although he would try telling himself later, when even he would sit up at night trying to reconcile what he had done with his image of himself, that his intentions weren't violent. He just wanted to scare her, maybe, or perhaps show her just how little power she actually had on this planet compared to him. There was no real reason or logic in his decision at all, but it felt perfectly right and just to him in the moment.

He started putting the suit on. If he moved quickly, he could still catch up.

20

Westin stood in the doorway next to Hartnup trying to make some sense of the situation. Nothing about what she had seen or heard so far from Hartnup set off an outright alarm in her head, but there was a dull buzz telling her something was off, and she had learned long ago that that sense needed to be listened to. It wasn't intuition, since Westin didn't believe in anything so vaguely New-Agey. It was more like she had seen all the clues she needed but hadn't yet put them in a logical order that would make them make sense. For every moment Hartnup stood next to her looking guilty, though, her mind was managing to put it all together.

"Was she here?" Westin asked as she stepped inside. She heard Hartnup follow her in, although the woman was absolutely quiet. Pretty typical for her, although to Westin she somehow seemed more quiet than normal.

Metzger stammered, his German accent stronger than normal. "I really don't…"

"*Was she here?*" Westin repeated.

"Um, yes." He pointed to the airlock. "She went out that way."

For a split second, Westin almost let her guard down. She was well aware of the despicable practice Svensson and one or two others had of forcing the working girls to actually walk out on the surface rather than be seen coming and going from his room. Crick leaving through the airlock seemed like a perfectly normal, if hardly reasonable, thing for her to do.

Except this is Metzger, Westin thought. He wasn't anywhere close to the disgusting slimebag Svensson was. If Crick left that way, it was because she had wanted to, not because it had been forced on her. And no one went outside unless they didn't have a choice. No one.

Westin turned to Hartnup. "Why was she here?"

"Uh, she was here for…" Hartnup gestured at Metzger as he zipped the front of his jumpsuit.

Westin took a step closer to her, forcing Hartnup to take a step back and stand flat against the wall. "No she wasn't."

"She was. Why else would…"

"If she was here just to fuck Metzger then you wouldn't be having trouble saying it, now would you? You are probably the least squeamish person when it comes to that in this entire colony short of the working girls themselves. So I'm going to ask you again and you better answer with the truth this time. Why. Was. She. Here?"

Hartnup hesitated, and Westin did the one thing she always told herself that she, the leader of over a hundred and fifty people trying to survive on a planet that every second was trying to kill them, would never do. She lost her cool.

"Fucking answer me!" Westin yelled.

Hartnup pulled herself even tighter against the wall, if that was even possible. Out of the corner of her eye, Westin saw Metzger flinch as well, followed by what looked like patting himself down. Westin turned to him just as he craned his neck trying to look down into his breast pocket.

She didn't need to ask. Westin knew very well what was supposed to be in that pocket.

She stalked out of Metzger's room and down the hall to her own room. Takibana stood just outside the door looking almost as confused as Metzger had.

"Tasha?" he asked. "What's going on? I thought you should know…"

"Go down to Metzger's room right now and arrest Leah Hartnup," Westin said.

"What for?"

"Conspiracy, maybe. I don't know and at this point I don't care. And I want you to…"

"Does this have something to do with the two people we're seeing outside?"

It wasn't until she stopped that Westin realized she had been pacing and chewing on her nails again. "What? What do you mean?"

"I just got a call from the security station. Cameras on the outside of the central building are picking up two environment suits. One's moving slow toward the main habitat wing. The other looks like it's running."

"I want all available security in the habitat wing. Cover all the public airlocks. Try to take anyone who comes in without making a big fuss."

"It'll be kind of hard," Takibana said. "People are going to notice. They'll start to get scared. Isn't that what you were trying to avoid?"

Westin thought long and hard about that. There was probably nothing else she could do. The truth about Earth was about to get out. She still had some options, though, on how that happened.

She also thought about that second environment suit, the one chasing the person who would obviously be Annabeth Crick. She tried to think who it might be and could only come up with one possibility, given how few airlocks there were between the administration wing and the habitat wing. She wasn't sure, though.

"You don't have an environment suit that fits you nearby, do you?" she asked.

"No, nearest one that comes close would be in the security station. Why?"

"Just go supervise the arrest. Remember, arrest the first two that come in, no matter what reason they may give for being out there."

"First two? Are there more that I'm not aware of yet?"

She walked over to her own airlock and the suit next to it. "Just one."

21

If there was one thing that anyone who had never set foot on Mars wouldn't be able to understand, it was the silence. Humans were used to ambient noise. What people thought of as silence was actually full of crickets chirping, wind rustling leaves, furnaces rumbling in the basement, the electric hum of appliances, distant voices or the whoosh of cars on freeways, birds chirping. Mars had none of this. Inside the colonies, true, there was enough sound in the background that a person wouldn't understand the silence of the dead world outside the thick walls and sealed airlocks. The inhabitants of the Rothschild colonies could even convince themselves that Mars didn't have a preternatural stillness when they heard a dust storm raging outside, the winds blowing hard enough against the outer walls that it could sound like the relentless pawing of enormous unfathomable beasts. Even the miners, who went out into the bleak landscape of Poynting Crater on a daily basis, didn't fully experience it. They had the whir and hum of their machinery and the persistent patter of their fellows trying to cover the quiet, whether they knew that was their true reasoning or not.

But Annabeth knew. The thin atmosphere on the red desert's surface meant that that very little sound carried from one place to another. On the rare occasions when she did hear something, usually a small stone that she might kick with her boot, the noise was muted even more so than the helmet over her ears could be blamed for. Unless someone was speaking to her directly through the suit's radio (something that wasn't as common in the emergency suits like this compared to the worker suits, and it appeared that, despite Metzger's importance, no one had sprung to equip him with one) all she could hear was the movement of her own hair in the helmet (caught in the tight suit enough that it made it difficult for her to even turn her head without feeling it painfully pulled), her breathing, and her pulse. That was a sound that had disturbed her the most the first several times she had been forced to walk outside, made all the more upsetting by the fact that she could hear it speed up as she had panicked. Those times had been the closest she'd ever experienced in her life to claustrophobia, and that was coming from someone who'd been locked in a tin can for nearly five months as she had hurtled through the void of space at ridiculous speeds to another planet.

Silence and loneliness. It was difficult to decide which one bothered her more on her walks back to her own section of habitat. The silence was disconcerting and it was always present. The feeling of being utterly alone hadn't come on to her until her third or fourth trek outside, yet when it did it had a far more heart-stopping feeling. She had imagined what it would be like wandering a desert back on Earth, no one to see her or help her if anything went wrong, and if her imagination had stopped there that would have been hard enough. Then she thought that, as alone as she might be in that situation back on her home planet, she still wouldn't truly be alone. In the immediate vicinity no matter where she was outside, even in the theoretical desert, there were other living things. If not vultures circling overhead or rodents burrowing beneath the sand then there were at least microscopic creatures, insects and mites and bacteria, living creatures that still managed to eke out an existence. Here that wasn't true. No other known living thing could live outside in this environment. Even the bacteria would die. Right here and now, she was the only living thing outside on the surface of the entire planet.

That was the sort of loneliness that could force a person to her knees and make her wonder if it was even worth carrying on. An existential crisis every time she came out onto the surface. She'd learned to recognize it and fight it, but it still made her move faster, desperate to get back inside the colony where she would no longer be able to think of such things.

Except getting back inside might present its own kind of crisis, now that she had the time to think about it. She'd gotten the PDA, but in her rush to do what she hoped was the right thing she hadn't thought what would come next. At some point, Metzger would realize it was missing, after all. If she were lucky, he wouldn't connect his missing hardware to her sudden and mysterious departure, but she doubted. He was naïve and trusting, but he wasn't an idiot no matter what anyone else might have said. He would figure it out. If she was lucky, though, he would also come to her about it first rather than security. Maybe by then Leah would have what she needed from it and Annabeth could give it back, passing off the whole thing as some kind of mistake.

She could feel the bulge of the PDA still in the sleeve of her jumpsuit. Its presence still gave her a horrible guilty feeling, even if she had managed to convince herself by not that Leah was right. Annabeth really hoped she would appreciate it, or at the very least not get mad at her for her improvisation. Still, given things Leah did for her like the underwear this morning, Annabeth had to...

She heard something move behind her.

Annabeth stopped, her heart suddenly beating faster even as she tried not to breathe, the breathes filling up her ears and preventing her from listening to what she was sure she had just heard. It had sounded like a rock skittering across the ground, as though had hit it accidentally and sent it flying. But she couldn't have heard it. It would have needed to be a relatively loud sound for her to catch it through the thin atmosphere and insulation of her environment suit. It could only be a figment of her imagination, a waking nightmare she had created for herself by dwelling on the planet's infinite loneliness for two long.

She heard the sound again. This time she felt something as well, a bump up against her heel as a rock had bounced over the ground and hit gently hit her.

A story came to her, one she had heard many years ago, and although she didn't know who had first written or said it, she knew it was often toted as the shortest horror story in the world: *The last man on Earth is sitting in a house. There's a knock at the door.*

"Knock knock," she whispered to herself. Slowly, very deliberately, Annabeth turned around.

Five feet away, so close she could have reached out and touched it, there was another environment suit. The visor was down, preventing her from seeing who was inside. They stood that way for several seconds, each staring at the other without being able to meet each other's eyes.

Then the mystery person in the environment suit charged right for her.

*

Svensson didn't notice the preternatural silence of the dead planet around him. He didn't care about the sprawling vistas of the perpetual red desert. When he went out his airlock, there was no sense of awe in him, nor loneliness, nor even much self awareness of what he was doing. All he felt was anger, not just as the slight perpetuated on him by that Crick bitch but at every tiny injustice and lack of respect and verbal jab he had received since coming to Mars. He had no idea what Crick was up to and he didn't care. He just wanted to put a good healthy fear in her. He wanted to make her acknowledge that he was her better. He might not have known how he was going to accomplish this, but he knew she wasn't going to go back inside Miranda until she learned the proper manners.

Once outside the airlock, he could see her ahead of him, still not yet halfway between the administration wing and the habit wing. There were many airlocks in both those wings, but only one on this side in between, an almost never-used emergency airlock leading to a hall in the commons wing. For whatever reason she was out here, he suspected she wouldn't be headed to that one. Whatever the hell she was doing couldn't be something she wanted others to know, and too many people would see her come in that way. She could only be heading to the habitat wing, probably the airlock right to her own apartment. At the slow and ponderous rate she was going, he believed he would have plenty of time to catch her.

The colony itself formed a half-moon shape, more or less matching the contour of the crater wall that slowly began sloping up on the other side of the colony, meaning that a straight walk from the administration wing to the habitat wing left a lot of empty and barren ground in between, the perfect area to come at her with no one else close by to interrupt. He dimly remembered as she moved across the wastes, in something less than a jog but more than a power-walk, that there would still be a few cameras on the outside that could see them, but he didn't feel particularly worried about that. Nothing on the outside of his suit identified him, and those cameras were barely watched on a regular basis anyways.

They were mostly there to keep an eye on weather conditions and monitor for damage to the colony's outer hulls. No one would notice him gaining quickly on that Crick bitch.

Running over the ground on Mars was hardly easy. It wasn't a smooth flat plain of red dust as so many movies of old had portrayed it. The surface was wildly uneven with small jagged rocks that prevented a straight dash right for Crick unless he wanted to risk a pair of broken ankles. Still, he gained on her quickly, mostly due to her overly cautious tread over the landscape. She still didn't turn back to see him approaching, and briefly he thought he would be able to overtake her without her suspecting a thing. At the last several meters, though, his foot struck a couple loose stones and sent the skittering ahead. He stopped dead in his tracks, hoping they wouldn't be enough for her to realize his presence, but they both hit the legs of her suit one after the other. She stopped, stood there for a moment, and then turned to look at him.

That's right. Now you're going to get it, he thought. He threw every thought of caution aside and ran right for her. She stumbled backward as he dove for her, causing both of them to sprawl to the ground as his hands brushed over her suit looking for purchase. They didn't find any, nor was he able to break his fall, but the lower gravity kept him from feeling little more than a bump as he face-planted. Svensson swore profusely as she thrashed about trying to get back up, except he wasn't used to maneuvering in an environment suit the way some others on the planet were. By the time he had managed to turn himself over and get back up to one knee, Crick was already completely back on her feet and doing an odd hobble-run for the habitat wing.

Neither of them had reason to look back in the direction they had come as one more airlock in the administration wing opened and released another suited figure.

*

Westin had been outside the colony only once since coming to Mars, and that was on the night she had arrived. New arrivals now had an airlock they could pass through to get inside the colony, but

Westin had been the second human being to set foot on the planet behind Takibana. The colony had been little more at the time than series of temporary inflatable labs and prefab habitats, all arrived ahead of the first settlers via unmanned supply drops. It wasn't until later, after much work and another shipment or two Miranda and the other colonies had begun to resemble their current state. Although the awe of being on another planet had hit her hard later, she hadn't waited outside longer than she had to. She'd been briefed more intensely than most on just what this planet could do to a human being in the elements.

Now here she was again, and just like last time there was no time to gape in awe. She could see the two suits from her current vantage point. She didn't know who the closer one might be, but the other had to be Crick. She had the PDA, but that didn't seem to matter at the moment. The much more important detail was that the second mystery suit was now running for her. Westin knew well enough that such a thing could only mean something truly bad.

Westin did her best bounding hop of a run over the nearest rocks, hoping to make up time and distance. If Crick made it to the airlock, she would be fine. Arrested, maybe, but fine. If the second figure caught up with her, though, there was no telling what it might do. She wished briefly that she had asked one of the security guards to come with her, but she hadn't thought there was time. She'd already understood that something bad was getting ready to happen outside, but trying to explain it would have taken valuable seconds. All of security would be waiting in the habitat wing, though, a fact that the second suited figure couldn't possibly know. All Westin had to do was make sure nothing came of either of them until they got there.

*

While her conscious thought wasn't coherent enough put the thought together in actual words, Annabeth knew that running across the empty landscape when she only had a limited supply of air was dangerous. None of the emergency suits were built for that kind of exertion. The suits the miners wore on a daily basis would be different, with large enough air tanks and internal filters to keep them out and working for eight hours or more at a time. Metzger's suit, on the other hand, was designed without the extra bulk, the better to get in on fast and then get to a different airlock in the event that one part of the colony lost air pressure. She didn't have the mathematical mind, however, to figure exactly how much air she was using as her lungs burned with each movement of her legs. She knew it wasn't a lot. She knew she needed to get to an airlock. Most importantly, she knew she needed to do it before the mystery person behind her caught up again.

She had no idea who was chasing her, and she didn't exactly care much just know. That could be figured out later. More important right now was to decide which airlock to go for. The closest at this point would have probably been the commons airlock, but that would have required her to turn and get around her attacker. That left the habitat wing, which was a little farther but offered many more airlocks. Almost all the two-person apartments were equipped with them, and there were two more connected to the smaller habitat modules. Any one would do. But first she had to make it there, and she could feel herself slowing as her body used up far more air than it was supposed to. The smaller filters in the emergency suit weren't designed to recycle this much carbon dioxide this quickly.

Even with her pursuer running flat out, she still couldn't hear the person, especially not over the ragged drumbeat of her pulse in her ears and wheezing of her own breath. She thought briefly to look behind her and see how close the person was, and if she were lucky they weren't even after her anymore, but she didn't dare. The helmet didn't provide her enough peripheral vision to see without turning almost completely around, and if her attacker were still right there that would be all the opportunity they would need.

There's the habitat wing, she thought. *Right there. Just a little more. Keeping pushing yourself. Another minute, maybe two, and you'll be...*

A thick gloved hand grabbed her by the shoulder and yanked.

*

Svensson stopped himself as abruptly as he could in the low gravity and low air pressure, pulling Crick with him. He felt his momentum trying to topple them both over again, yet he caught his balance at the last moment and stayed upright. Crick wasn't so lucky. The force of his pull on her shoulder brought her down back first on a large jagged rock, and even with no mikes in their suits and only the thinnest atmosphere between them, Svensson could hear her scream in agony as it jabbed into her spine. Dimly, he thought that maybe that was enough, that the little bit of pain and whole lot of fear he had caused her would be enough to keep her in line in the future, except red fury still clouded his vision. No, that most definitely would not be enough. He had to do more. He had to make her pay. He had to finally make someone respect him.

He pushed her off the rock with his boot and rolled her over onto her side. As he stooped lower to get a closer look, he thought he heard a faint hissing. He prodded her suit a couple times until he saw the sound's likely source. There was a very small hole in the bulky back part of her suit. Right about the location of her air supply. A tiny white vapor curled out into the air but vanished from sight before it could get far from the suit. One of the air tanks must have been punctured.

Okay, that's enough, he thought. *Had my fun, time to go back inside.*

Except it didn't have to be over. The leak didn't have to mean anything. He could keep her here until the last moment and then let her go back. Besides, there was no way she was scared enough yet. At this point, she might still try to report this to security when she was back within the safety of those pre-fab polymer walls. She could still easily forget the terror of being out in the emptiness all alone with no one to help her. He had to make sure she understood completely that she could never mess with him ever again.

But she can't even see who I am, he thought. It was one of the only moments of rational thought he'd had within the last five minutes. His gold visor was still down, protecting his eyes from the harsh glare of the waning Martian day and keeping anyone on the outside from getting a clear view in. The same held true for her. He couldn't see the pure terror that was likely on her face.

Svensson couldn't really teach her the lesson if she didn't see for certain that it was him, and his own enjoyment doing it this way was muted. He would have to bring her back to his apartment if he wanted this to end in any way in his favor.

Annabeth sluggishly moved on the ground. Without seeing her face, Svensson couldn't tell if her minimal movement was because she was unconscious or in pain or anything else. Whatever the cause, it meant that hopefully she wouldn't be able to fight him off. He bent down to pick her up, expecting her to be light and easy to throw around in the low gravity, but he never got the chance to find out for sure. Something slammed into his helmet from behind, and again he found himself sprawled out face first in the dirt and rocks.

The shock kept him in that position for too many precious seconds before he forced himself back to his hands and knees. A glance to his side showed that Annabeth was no longer there, but she couldn't have gone far. The limited peripheral vision of the helmet kept him from seeing what had hit him, though, and he figured that was the more important thing to discern right now. Bringing first one foot up and to the ground, then the other, he stood straight and turned.

There were two environment suits now standing out here with him in the frozen desert. One of them would be Annabeth, while he had no clue who the other might be. He wasn't even sure which was which. Both of them were newer models, the kind that could only come from the administration wing, and from the shape of their chests both were clearly women. They also both had their visors down. Suddenly Svensson wasn't so sure he could recognize Annabeth purely by her chest after all.

He hesitated for several moments, unsure how to proceed. The rage still drove him, but he was able to think just clearly enough to know that two witnesses would make his chance of getting away with this that much harder.

No, don't you fucking be like that, he thought to himself. *You can't let her get away with this just because she has a friend with her.*

Wait. A friend. He suddenly understood who this had to be. Annabeth was now standing with Leah Hartnup. It was the only person who could possibly have been idiotic enough to come out here and challenge him. It was all just another way to humiliate him, to make him look small. Well fuck that. He wasn't going to let them get away with this.

No. Run. Get back inside. This is getting out of hand. A small voice of reason kept trying to cajole him back to his airlock, but it wasn't enough to be heard over his fury. Screw scaring these schmucks. The only way to teach them both a lesson now was to make sure they actually got hurt.

Svensson rushed them. One stumbled behind the other, her slow movements making him think that one must have been Crick. He didn't care which one he was targeting now, though. Either one was a far target. He expected Hartnup try to get out of his way as well, but rather than a full on retreat she dodged slightly to the right, allowing Svensson's own momentum to carry him past her. As their suits brushed, Hartnup raised her hands up, clasping them together as best she could in the bulky gloves, and brought them down hard on Svensson's back. He made an *oof* sound that was impossibly loud within the confines of his suit and again almost lost his balance. He pinwheeled his arms until he was sure he wouldn't fall over, then turned to look at her.

One of the suits, likely Crick, was running away to the habitat wing. At this point, Svensson was no longer even considering catching her because the other stood in front of him, taking what might have been the bulky suit, low-gravity version of a fighting stance. She'd hit him. She'd actually hit him.

Nobody should have been allowed to hit him. He was the goddamned production manager. He was important. He mattered. Neither of these pieces of shit had the right to touch him.

There was no more room for a voice of reason in his head.

He threw a punch at Hartnup, and this time she didn't dodge in time. It hit her square in the chest, but the padding of the suit muted the blow. She got her arms up in time to block the next two punches before getting in her own shot right to his kidney. Again, though, the suit kept the punch from feeling like anything more than a hard shove. They both tried to circle each other, but the terrain and low gravity made balance during such a delicate dance difficult. She threw another punch, hitting him in the helmet, but he got the impression that she was pulling it a little. Of course, he realized, she didn't want to actually hurt him or damage his suit. She wasn't doing this fight for any other reason than to give Crick a chance to escape. There was no actual malice on her part.

Svensson couldn't say the same thing.

He swung again twice, thinking he was starting to get the hang of a fight in such an abnormal setting, yet she managed to dodge again both times. When he left her open for her own shot, she didn't go for his chest or head anymore, this time awkwardly swinging her thick-booted foot at his groin. It connected and sent him falling to his knees, but not out of pain. He barely felt the impact between the suit's padding and the kick's slow speed, instead dropped yet again because of balance. The kick proved to be far more disastrous for her, as he grabbed her boot in his fall and twisted. The other foot left the ground and she fell straight on her back in an almost slow motion move that might have been comical under any other circumstances.

Svensson took only a second to catch his breath. He hadn't been prepared for this kind of exertion with so little oxygen at his disposal, but any thoughts of breathing vanished as he saw her there, flat on her back and obviously stunned, with the exact same rock that punctured Crick's air sitting right next to her.

He didn't think. He only felt. Revenge. Anger. Paranoia. Embarrassment. All these things came together in this moment.

Svensson grabbed the red rock, surprisingly light, and lifted it over his head. There was a single brief moment of clarity, that little voice in his head saying the single word "no," before it was run over by all the other mangled thoughts rushing forward.

As hard as he could manage he brought the rock down directly onto Hartnup's chest. She jerked under the impact but it hadn't felt to him like the blow had done anything. He brought it up and down again, willing his muscles to do it even harder this time, and now he felt like something gave way under the suit, something solid cracking under the pressure. And yet it still wasn't enough. She brought up her hands to protect her chest even as Svensson aimed higher, bashing the rock against her neck. She immediately began flailing about, but he couldn't tell if it was because he had done damage to her windpipe or she was trying to find some purchase to get out from under his onslaught. Either way, he didn't care. He smashed the rock into her visor, an action that didn't appear to do much more than scratch the surface. This only made him more furious, and he hit her faceplate again and again and again. She hit him repeatedly in the chest, but he barely felt any of the attacks. Each attempt to get him away from her was a little more feeble than the last. He didn't notice. All he cared about was the way her visor seemed to resist his attacks, like even her suit itself refused to give him the respect he deserved. It became just another thing that needed to pay. The people of the colony, the colony itself, the very planet beneath them. Every single thing needed to pay, and all that irrational hatred became focused on the single point of her helmet beneath his rock. Over. And over. And over.

A crack spider-webbed across her visor.

The rock came down again.

Her fingers batted ineffectively at his chest.

The rock came down again.

Inside his suit, Svensson sweated. He panted. And he smiled.

The rock came down again. The gold plastic shattered.

The sound was muted, but there was no mistaking it for anything other than an explosion as the final blow caused the visor to shatter outward rather than in. The greater pressure from inside the suit threw the plastic shards right at Svensson, and as he jerked away all his red rage bleached away to become sudden, incapacitating fear. No. He hadn't just done that. He couldn't have. It hadn't been him, not really. It couldn't have. He wasn't the kind of person who could...

He fell back on his ass and scooted away from her flailing form as quickly as he could. Her hands groped helplessly at her helmet as though there were still some way she could close it against the alien elements, but except for some shards around the side there was nothing there, no hole that could be plugged long enough for her to get back to an airlock. Briefly Svensson thought *I have to do something*, but what was there to do? The suite injected emergency sealant into any tears in the event of a rip, but there was nothing that could fix what he had done. There was no way he could pick her up and run her back to the colony in time to do anything.

So instead he just sat there and stared as she jerked and twisted and writhed, her action slowing down with every passing second until finally she stopped, her hands falling flat on the ground beside her helmet and her feet, which had been pounding the ground to release small clouds of dust to float lazily in the sky, finally ending their staccato drumbeat.

He sat there staring for nearly a minute before the truth of what he had done would enter his shocked brain. He had just murdered Leah Hartnup.

Standing back up was a slow process. Twice he tried and found that his legs wouldn't support him. Idly he wondered for a moment if the exertion in such an extreme environment had done something to him, but he didn't feel like anything was wrong with his body now that he breathing was calming and his heart wasn't beating quite as fast. It didn't slow down to a normal rate yet, though. He was pretty sure only a psychopath could have accomplished such a feat, and he didn't think he was one. Then again, how could he be sure given what he had just done?

On his third try, he managed to stand again, but he wouldn't yet look at Hartnup's face. He wanted to see what the open air of Mars had done to her, and yet he didn't. He'd always felt a vague loathing for her, much like he felt for a number of people, but he had never thought he would want her dead. He knew he had to look eventually, though. He needed to see without question what he had done. Then, once that was over with, he could begin figuring out some kind of cover story.

He stood there facing away from her for another minute, waiting for his heart to slow even further, before he finally turned and looked down at the ruin in her helmet.

Svensson saw it all without understanding at first. He saw the way her eyes, still open even in death, bulged in her head. He didn't know if that was from the lack of oxygen or the thin atmosphere or some other biological occurrence, nor was he sure he cared. Her skin was tinged blue, again maybe because of the freezing air or instead the lack of oxygen. There was a strange crystalline formation on her lips that took several seconds for him to figure out. That was her spit, he realized. She'd started foaming at the mouth in the last seconds of her life, and a combination of the atmosphere and the temperature had done strange things to her saliva. Even now some of it seemed to be disappearing as the moisture changed to gas and vanished into the literal thin air.

This he saw. What he did not see at first, at least not until his mind forced him to make sense of her strange features, was that this was not in fact Leah Hartnup. Nor was it Annabeth Crick.

Svensson turned and ran back to his own airlock, any potential thoughts of bringing the body in or otherwise hiding it disappearing as only one word repeated itself over and over in his head.

Jarvla, jarvla, jarvla, jarvla, jarvla…

Fuck.

He had just murdered Tasha Westin.

22

Leah wasn't in Metzger's room anymore when security came for her, but she didn't think it would be long before they found her. Miranda was a closed, cramped environment. It wasn't designed for running and hiding. Even if she got creative, she would be found within a half hour. But she didn't think she needed a half hour. She only needed enough time to meet Annabeth at an airlock, then a little bit more to get into Metzger's PDA and find this secret that administration so desperately wanted no one else to know.

She knew this was a mistake. She knew this wouldn't accomplish anything anymore. And she also knew that she couldn't go through all this rigmarole just to be denied the truth at the last moment. She was screwed. She knew that and she couldn't change it. She was probably going back to Earth a pauper, maybe even with a one way ticket back to jail. But damn it if she wasn't going to find some way to declare victory anyway.

Making it out of the administration wing was easier than she had expected. Although she was sure security would be looking for her, she heard some commotion from somewhere behind her as Takibana and his people shouted something about video cameras. They were probably trying to watch Annabeth and figure out where she would be coming back in. Although she knew that would be the first place security would look for her, Leah ran through the halls of the commons wing back to her own apartment in the habitat wing. Annabeth wouldn't know that their entire plan was blown, after all, and that would be where she would likely come back in. Leah could only hope that she would make it before security.

She ignored all the odd looks the others gave her as she ran, but again there weren't nearly as many odd looks as she expected. In the exercise room, one of the few places in the commons wing that had port holes to view outside, she saw multiple people gathered around the windows. That almost slowed Leah. A single person trudging out on the surface shouldn't have been anything to watch. They'd all seen it countless times before. Leah thought for a moment that a storm had suddenly blown in and they were watching the lone figure in her environment suit brave the red dust clouds, except Schwartzman the meteorologist would have made an announcement about that over the intercoms before it happened. A storm on Mars, whether they were inside or out, was something everyone wanted to be prepared for on the chance it could cause some serious damage to their survival chances.

Whatever it was, Leah couldn't get distracted. It was too likely that the minutes she had left of her freedom were slowly vanishing with every moment she waited.

She slowed a little in the habitat wing. Most of the two person apartments here had an airlock as well as two of them in the halls connecting the habitat modules. Annabeth could theoretically come in through any one of them. If this had been Earth, the entrances to the personal quarters from outside would have had locks on them, but with so few people there was little reason to fear crime, and in the event of emergencies safety dictated that someone outside should be able to get through any of them. But Leah couldn't wait in the hall listening for any commotion to indicate where she was coming in. She needed to be there when Annabeth came through. Finally, she decided her own apartment was the best option. Yes, that would be where everyone would look for her first. It was also the most likely place Annabeth would come through if she didn't realize there was a problem, and one of the closer airlocks if she did.

While the door to her apartment could lock from the inside for privacy, Leah didn't bother with it. Security would have the codes to get in if they really wanted to. She thought for a second about trying to pull some of the sparse furniture to block the door, but that would only buy her seconds, considering how small most of the items in the room were. All she could do was sit and wait, hoping that Annabeth came in first.

Leah sat on the bottom bunk, Annabeth's bunk, and prepped herself for the long arduous minutes it would take for either one or the other the door open. Now that she had time to think, she had time to second guess her decision.

I hope you think this was worth it, Leah, she thought. *Five years living on this hellhole planet, all ruined.*

No, it was worth it. She knew it. Or at least she tried to tell herself she knew it. Whatever was going on had to be important. It had to be done now. If she'd waited who knew what would have happened.

What would have happened probably wasn't even any of your business.

But it had to be. It had to be something important to the whole colony, right?

It's probably dark Syndicate matters you never really wanted to see. Just like what you suspect happened to Max Perrish. And that's probably where you're going next. The incinerators of Rochelle, or a shallow grave next time they send out automated diggers to lay down com lines between here and Kurtis. Curiosity killed the cat, Leah.

"But satisfaction brought her back," she murmured. How many times in her life had she repeated that line to herself, she had to wonder? Too many to count. And how many times had the satisfaction just not been worth it? By her rough estimate, maybe half the time. But she doubted anything she might or might not be about to uncover would kill her. Information had never harmed anybody. Nobody was dying today on Mars.

Getting locked up, however, was a completely different story.

I wonder if they're going to keep me in that tiny cell for my remaining months before they send me back, Leah thought. That would suck. The few tiny cells in security weren't intended for long-term use and were much smaller than her cell had been back on Earth. *Maybe they'll just lock me in here, although that might be difficult with Annabeth still...*

Still doing what? Still turning tricks? Would they really still allow Annabeth to do her job after helping steal vital administration secrets? For the first time, it dawned on Leah just how screwed Annabeth was right along with Leah.

"Oh God, what have I done?" Leah whispered. Maybe Annabeth would continue on as a working girl and maybe she wouldn't, but she would probably be going back home just like Leah. Her financial situation had been more tenuous than Leah's from the get-go, but now she would be worse off than ever. She would be incredibly lucky if she could ever get her job reheating hamburgers back, not to mention the fact that she might be going to jail as well.

I've ruined her, Leah thought. It was one thing to do this to herself, but she'd destroyed her best friend in the process. Leah had been able to forgive herself for a hell of a lot in her life, yet she could never look herself in the mirror now.

Idly she thought about marching right back out her door and down to the security offices. She could still maybe make some of this right. She could claim she'd tricked Annabeth, that Annabeth hadn't had any clue what she was being asked to do. She stood up to do just that when she heard a bang from the outer wall. Too late now. Annabeth was here.

Leah went over to the airlock door and waited for the heavy polymer composite to slide open. They were at a point now where every second would count. She would need to get the PDA and start with possible passwords immediately. If the PDA's security was set to lock her out completely after a certain number of failed attempts, she might be in trouble. Under other circumstances where she had more time she might find a way around that, but for now she simply had to hope she was right that Metzger would use a simple password. And then, if that worked and she got in...

Well, she would have her answer to all this mystery, but she wouldn't know what to do with it. Not that she would have enough time and freedom left to do something anyway.

As she stood there thinking about this, she heard the outer door slide open and, a few seconds later, close again. Had she been less distracted she might have noticed right away that the timing between the first and second sound was off, that more time had elapsed than should have been necessary for Annabeth to walk in and hit the "close" button. As the seconds ticked by and Leah didn't hear the mechanical humming of air cycling back into the airlock, though, she finally began to realize something was wrong.

"Annabeth?" she asked. "Annabeth, is something wrong? Can you hear me?" She realized that was a stupid question as soon as it was out of her mouth. Until a breathable atmosphere was pumped back in, the air would be too thin to carry more than the barest of sound waves. She knocked, again realizing only after that such an action was also pointless. If this had been one of the airlocks in the administration wing she would have had two portholes, one on the inside door and one on the outside, but the airlocks in the habitat wing had been made by different contractors for cheaper. The only way to understand what was going on beyond this door was to open it.

She hit the button that cycled the air back in, fidgeting nervously as she waited for the light next to the button to glow green. A part of her was still thinking about how long before she was hauled away, but with each passing moment more and more horrible thoughts came to her about what had gone wrong. She remembered the faulty latch on Annabeth's Russian-made surplus suit, but there couldn't be anything wrong with this one. It was one of the administration's suits, after all. They would never give one of the higher-ups something faulty, right?

The light turned green. Leah hit the open button. Annabeth was face down on the floor of the airlock, not moving.

Leah fell to her knees beside Annabeth and turned her over, screaming at her to be okay, to not have anything wrong. She pried off the catches on Annabeth's helmet to find the woman blue in the lips, her breathing shallow, her eyes closed. No matter how much Leah shook her, Annabeth's eyes refused to open.

That was when security finally came in.

23

Svensson knew where all the cameras were on the outside of Miranda, and after a minute of running back to his own airlock for over a minute, his paranoid brain finally took over from the part that was acting on blind panic.

There may not be any camera pointed directly at my airlock, but they'll be able to tell the direction I'm going. If I head right for my own room they'll figure out who did it. Was it even possible that he could get away with this? That didn't seem at all likely to him, but *not likely* and *not possible* were two different things. If he stopped, if he focused, if he completely embraced that part of himself that always thought everyone was out to get him, then maybe he could get through this unscathed. Because for once, really and truly with no exaggeration, every person on Mars really would be out to get him.

The first order of business was to get out of the range of every camera. Despite his desperate desire get back inside out of the hellscape sooner rather than later, Svensson made sure that he, within full view of one of the cameras, walked off away from the colony rather than toward it until he was positive he was out of sight. Then he came back in, this time in one of the blind spots, until he was up against one of the walls of the administration wing. From here, he might be able to work his way back around to his own apartment. Most of the cameras wouldn't be pointed right down at the wall beneath them, after all. They would be pointing in the direction of the mining operation or the approach from Kurtis or whatever. But he also suspected that might be the same direction security would go in searching for the murderer. He hadn't been terribly stealthy in his approach on Crick, after all. So no, not his own apartment.

Keeping tight to the walls the whole time, Svensson made his way all around the administration wing and to the support wing. Given how incredibly important every single thing in this wing was to the colony, there were a lot more cameras here. It was the beating heart of Miranda, the place where the water plant was located, the air filters, the power relay where Miranda joined up with the underground cables from Kurtis and Rochelle. It was also the first part of Miranda that had ever been constructed, much of it in the early days when large parts of the work had to be done outside with little that could be done inside. There were more airlocks in this area than any other besides the habitat wing, and few of them were ever opened anymore except for the one that pointed out on the landing zone and the much larger lock used for the transport rover to Kurtis. Svensson made his way as far as he could among the tangle of angles provided by the cameras to the nearest airlock he didn't think would be watched. He hit the button for the outer door and walked in. It took twenty or thirty seconds for the atmosphere to cycle back into the room, forcing him to finally confront what he had just done.

No, I didn't do anything, he thought. *It wasn't my fault. Westin should have never been there. This was none of her business.*

He understood the truth of that. Westin brought her death upon herself for interfering is something Svensson clearly had the right to do. Except he doubted he could get anyone else to come around to his way of thinking. It was simply in their nature to be mediocre, to not comprehend the ways of their betters. The only choice he had now was to do everything in his power to cover it up.

The green light lit up and Svensson cautiously pressed the button to open the inner door. Security would be looking for someone, yes, but they wouldn't know where to start. There weren't enough of Takibana's people to watch every way in. The airlock he had chosen led him into the hall directly outside the water plant, which he had known would be sparsely populated at this time of day. Thankfully, there was no one waiting for him and no one to accidentally see him. So he was back in. But what else did he need to do to ensure his safety?

He looked down at his environment suit. It was absolutely covered in reddish dust from his scuffle with Westin and Crick. The only people who would usually look this dirty coming back in were the miners themselves. If anyone saw the suit in its current condition, they would realize instantly that he was the mysterious brawler who had killed the colony's leader. He needed to wash it. Or, he realized, get rid of it completely. He had no idea what other evidence he might have brought in with him. There could be micro-tears on his gloves from the rock he had used or traces of Westin's DNA or whatever. He didn't know enough about investigative procedures to even be sure what to look for. Svensson needed to hide the suit, or better yet destroy it if he could find a way.

Now wasn't the time for that, though. It suddenly occurred to him that the longer it took for anyone else to see him the more likely his absence would be noted. His only choice was to stash the suit quickly for now. He could come back later and figure out how to get rid of the evidence.

The inside of the water plant was quiet for now, although he knew he couldn't be completely alone. There would be a control booth nearby where a technician was always present and monitoring the automated operations. The booth would have windows looking out in the plant's largest room at the various cisterns inside, but Svensson knew from experience that there were corners behind the cisterns that were out of view and rarely used except by people looking for a quiet place to perhaps do something they shouldn't. Svensson sneaked into the nearest of these corners and hurriedly removed the suit, then shoved it behind some of the metal latticework that surrounded the pumps and machinery at the bottom of one of the cisterns. He'd have to come back soon. Mandatory preventative maintenance required that someone look under there at least once every six sols.

With the suit hidden and Svensson back to wearing nothing but his jumpsuit, he made his way down the hall, trying as hard as possible not to look like he was up to something despite his sweat-drenched forehead and clothes. As he got back to the commons wing, he found everyone in a state of chaos and panic. Everyone knew something bad was going on, yet no one knew what. Among it all Svensson didn't look at all suspicious.

I can do this, he thought. *I can get away with it.* And now, he realized, with Westin gone he might be able to get away with a whole lot more. Metzger was not fit to run this colony. There would be a void in leadership. With the right moves, the right planning, maybe even the right flat out lies, Svensson could be the one filling that void.

Yeah. Maybe I can. I can lead. People will respect me. I'll finally make *them respect me.*

Despite the general sense of disorder swirling around everyone he passed, Svensson found himself whistling cheerily.

24

They didn't take Leah to any of the cells. Instead, on Takibana's orders, Haruma Matsumoto and Monique Kristfal stood guard over her with their stun guns as she followed the people who'd been conscripted to take Annabeth the clinic. Leah was thoroughly confused by this, especially the fact Takibana apparently had something more pressing than this to deal with elsewhere, but she was grateful. Every time she tried to ask the two guards what was happening they stonewalled her, Kristfal with angry cussing and Matsumoto with just a bewildered shake of her head.

Leah was forced to wait on a bench just outside the clinic proper, though, as Doctor and Nurse Lipschitz ran in and immediately went to work on Annabeth. Leah wanted to try pushing her way past the guards and through the door just so that she could be by Annabeth's side, especially if this was the poor woman's final moments, but she understood just how thin the ice that she stood on already was. She was a criminal. If they hadn't understood the full extent of it before then they would the instant they peeled the environment suit off Annabeth's body and found the PDA wherever she'd hidden it. She was going to be punished in some way soon, and she knew she would deserve it. In fact, if Annabeth died, she was fully prepared to accept charges of murder. Leah might not have had any idea what had happened outside to damage Annabeth's suit (and it had become clear to her, as she'd held Annabeth in her arms and tried to make sense of this, that there had been a puncture in the suit right over the air supply), but she knew that Annabeth wouldn't have even been out there if Leah hadn't roped her into this little scheme. And all for what? Well, Leah probably would never know now. For all she knew, it had been something petty - Kleinstock's absence would be for some mundane reason, the mysterious recording for Sandeep Benegal would have been altered for something minor, and none of this would have mattered in the slightest.

She was so lost in her own tears and shame that she didn't

notice the passage of time, nor did she hear much of the muttering beyond the clinic door as the Lipschitzes did their best to save their patient. The one thing she couldn't ignore, though, was the commotion down the hall when nearly all the remaining security guards appeared. There were people following behind them, whispering and swearing and crying, and Takibana yelled for all of them to back away, often slipping back into his native Japanese for what Leah was sure had to be cuss words. The guards were tight in the cramped corridor, and for a moment Leah wondered why they didn't just give each other some space when she realized they were carrying something between them, something large and unwieldy that required all of them to work together despite the low gravity. As they came closer, she saw it was an environment suit, covered in Martian dust and supported on a stretcher from some emergency closet.

Leah stood up to get a better look as they passed, mindful of the way her two guards fidgeted with their weapons at her movement. They both looked to Takibana as though expecting some order to subdue her, yet he didn't pay the three of them any attention. Instead, Leah realized, he was rubbing his eyes, trying to hide tears that still managed to slip out from under his hand and down his cheeks.

As the stretcher passed her and went through the door, Leah looked down at the smashed faceplate of the suit's helmet and understood why. The group of security personnel closed the clinic door behind them, leaving Leah to gape at the unexpected turn of events.

This was just supposed to be another day when I woke up this morning, Leah thought. *One day closer to going back to Earth. How the absolute flying fuck to it all go so bloody pear-shaped?*

Her mind was blank for the rest of her wait outside the clinic. There was too much going on for her to process any of it. Even though she continued to cry, her mind refused to think on everything. She only dimly realized there was a computer term that perfectly summed her up at the moment, the one used when a computer catastrophically crashed. BSOD. Blue Screen of Death.

Various security people came and went from the clinic. Dimly, in the back of her brain, Leah kept track of them, registering that more were leaving than were coming, until finally the corridor was quiet again except for the breathing of her captor and the sound of her heart rumbling in her ears. She was staring down at her hands in her lap when a shadow appeared over her. Leah looked up to see Takibana. His face was a complicated mask of emotions that Leah couldn't completely read. A deep sadness certainly seemed among, possibly with a large amount of rage. But when he spoke his voice was calm and even, the constant professional.

"You can go in to see Crick now."

"What happens after that?" Leah asked.

"There are a large number of things I would like to do," he said. He pulled a hand from behind his back and showed her Metzger's PDA. It was only inches from her face now yet she would never find out what secrets it kept. All of this chaos and confusion for nothing. "But that's not my call."

"Who's call is it?"

"Met..." He paused in the middle of Metzger's name, then sighed. "Damned if I know. Go in. I'm keeping Matsumoto on the door though, so don't try anything. You're going to give a statement soon, once we figure some things out." Nothing about his last sentence suggested it was a friendly request. Leah nodded, and he turned to walk away.

The inside of the clinic matched the disheveled state of Leah's mind. Anil Khan was still in one of the beds, but he'd been moved to the farthest corner and had a curtain drawn around him, as though he'd been shoved aside and forgotten in the bedlam. The lone operating table was on the other side of the room, and despite the dead body lying on top of it, that whole area also felt abandoned. Leah allowed a moment of horrified curiosity to take over, a part of her chiding herself for letting that blasted emotion control her yet again, and she took a few steps closer to the body just to be certain she hadn't been seeing things earlier. But no, she'd been right the first time. Tasha Westin was inside the suit, very obviously dead.

"Don't touch that... er, her. Don't touch her," Nurse Lipschitz said. She was on a stool near the door, so quiet and still that Leah had walked right past her without noticing. "Takibana just needed somewhere to put her for now so we can, uh, investigate later."

By investigate Leah was sure she meant "autopsy." As far as Leah was aware, that particular procedure had never been needed on Mars before. From the look of Westin, the cause of death was obvious, yet Leah was sure that this had to have something to do with whatever had happened to Annabeth's suit as well. This hadn't just been some freak accident. Annabeth had gone out and Westin had apparently gone out after her, except Leah didn't think that made much sense. There wouldn't have been a reason for Westin to go out unless there'd been some other factor.

Of course, none of that was what really mattered to Leah just now. Instead, Leah searched out the clinic's two other beds. Annabeth was in one, blankets over her and pulled up to her breast. Her jumpsuit had been pulled apart at the chest. A defibrillator next to her bed told the story of what had been needed to save her life. Her environment suit was discarded on the bed next her, looking eerily close to the dead body not ten feet away.

Dr. Lipschitz stood over Annabeth, adjusting a breathing tube in Annabeth's mouth. There was also an IV in her arm and multiple tubes and wires running to various points on her body. Annabeth had her eyes closed but the steady rhythm of lines on a nearby monitor told Leah quite clearly that her best friend was still alive.

"Miss Hartnup," Dr. Lipschitz said to her with a nod.

"Is she going to be okay?" Leah asked.

Dr. Lipschitz's white bearded mouth twisted in an expression that could only be described as bemused. "When people asked me that question back on Earth it was, in most cases, something I could answer easily. Here though?" He looked down at Annabeth as though she could be the one to answer. She didn't move. "As far as I can tell, she wasn't breathing for something around eleven minutes. Her heart was stopped for two or three. Leah, I don't know if she's going to wake up. If she does, I'm almost certain there will be some degree of brain damage. But we don't have the right equipment to diagnose this kind of thing."

"Billions and billions of dollars to put people on Mars, and not a few more dollars for medical supplies," Leah muttered.

"Supplies aren't the issue. Shipping an MRI machine over millions of miles of space, though, takes time and energy the Syndicate preferred to use on mining equipment. For only a hundred and fifty odd people, they probably didn't think it was the highest priority."

"So where does that leave her, then?" Leah asked.

"We won't know until she wakes up."

"If she wakes up," Leah whispered, not fully wanting to admit it to herself.

"If she wakes up," Dr. Lipschitz agreed.

"Can I be alone with her?" Leah asked.

"We can try to give you some space, at least," he said. Leah nodded. It wasn't like she could ask for more than that. The Lipschitzes lived in a small room just off the clinic, and there weren't many other places for them to go. Nurse Lipschitz offered Leah her stool, which Leah pulled over to the side of Annabeth's bed as the Lipschitzes both moved on to Westin's body. They talked quietly to each other while Leah held her friend's hand. It felt very cold to the touch, but if Leah moved her hand to the woman's wrist she could just barely feel her pulse.

"Annabeth," Leah said quietly. She hoped doctor-patient privilege extended to anything she might say while sitting here, although she supposed it didn't matter if the Lipschitzes heard her anyway. News of Leah's little scheme would likely spread throughout Miranda one way or the other, especially if it was decided that it had in some way contributed to Westin's death. If that turned out to be true, Leah understood she was no longer simply looking at being shipped back to Earth as a pauper. She was looking a possibility, however small, of a short trip out an airlock without a suit.

And yet Leah couldn't bring herself to care about such a possibility anymore. If that's what was decided, she would accept it. But she would be much more willing to go along with it if she were somehow able to believe that her sacrifice would keep Annabeth alive. She wasn't religious, although nominally she belonged to the Church of England. Right now, though, she almost wanted to pray to God to take her instead of her friend.

"I messed up, Annabeth. When I came to Mars, I told myself I wasn't going to be that person anymore, the one who can't stop poking her nose where it doesn't belong. Then I did it, and here you are. I'm sorry. I'm so, so sorry." Leah's breath hitched as a fresh wave of tears rolled down her cheeks. "Please don't die. You're the only friend I have here. You're the only friend I have anywhere."

"Not even Dr. Ruiz?" someone asked from the clinic's door. Both of the Lipschitz's stopped whispering. Leah didn't have to look to see who it was. She'd expected that voice to come for her soon.

"Martin and I have an arrangement. That's really all it is between us." Leah sucked in a deep breath and turned around on her stool. Metzger stood there, although something about the way he held himself made him look much taller than usual. "Is Takibana waiting outside to take me to a cell?"

"If he was, would you go or would you fight it?"

Leah held her hands up in front of her, fists tightly balled and wrists together as though ready to have handcuffs slapped on them. Not that there were handcuffs on Mars beyond the pair that Weasel claimed she had sold to a husband and wife in Rochelle, but Metzger looked like he understood the gesture just the same.

Metzger nodded once, but he didn't come for her. Instead, he took a couple steps toward Westin's body. "Do you think you two can go to the commons wing for a few minutes?" he asked the Lipschitzes. "I need a moment with both Miss Hartnup and Miss Westin."

"Just so you're aware, Anil Khan is still here as well," Nurse Lipschitz said.

As if in answer, Khan snored from behind his curtain. That was enough of a response for everyone, and the Lipschitzes left.

Metzger hesitated for several moments before walking over to Westin's body. He looked down at the broken faceplate and the horror show beneath, but to Leah's surprise he didn't flinch. He didn't even show much emotion at all. "I know how people around here think of me, you know." Leah wasn't sure whether he was addressing the corpse or her until he looked up and met her eyes. "They don't know how someone like me becomes second-in-command of one of the greatest endeavors ever attempted by man. And honestly, neither do I. Someone decided this was the place for me, and I've been trying to be a person others could believe in. I don't think even Westin thought that was likely." He nodded in

Annabeth's direction. "She did, though. Or at least she made me think she did. Yes, I understand that was part of her job, to make a person's fantasy come true, but doesn't it say something that she at least knew my fantasy was to be treated like I was respected?"

Leah didn't think he wanted an actual answer to that, which was fine because she didn't know what could possibly be said. He looked down into Westin's face for a minute longer before pulling a towel from a nearby shelf and draping it over the ruined helmet. It suddenly occurred to Leah that a large number of people had already been in and out of this room since the body had been brought in, yet no one before now had thought to give Westin that tiny amount of dignity.

Once he was satisfied with the towel's placement, Metzger walked over to join Lean at Annabeth's side. They both stared at her silently for several minutes before he spoke again. "There might be some debate whether I have control over the other two colonies, or even this one given the temperament of some of the other senior staff members. But for now, I'm in charge of Miranda, and I'm saying that you're not going to be arrested. I think I understand why you tried to do what you did."

Leah gulped. If she didn't know Metzger, she would have thought he was toying with her in some way. "You're not going to discharge me back to Earth?"

"No one is getting sent back to Earth," he said. There was something strange about the cadence of how he said it, as though there were clearly supposed to be some kind of hidden meaning that Leah just didn't get.

"Not even the person who did this to Annabeth and Westin?"

"Takibana will find who did this." He paused with an expression on his face like the very idea of thinking long and hard about something was difficult, then he nodded as though coming to a decision. With no further word, he reached into the breast pocket of his jumpsuit and pulled out his PDA.

"I took this back from Takibana." He held it out to her.

Leah hesitated to take it, partially expecting it to shock her or cause more general havoc if she touched it. "I don't understand."

"What is the saying that Americans have? I cannot take my brain out of the coffin?"

Leah puzzled over that for a second before realizing what he meant. "You mean you can't think outside the box."

"That's it. Westin used to say that, usually about me when she didn't think I was listening. But unfortunately, today I think she was the one with her head in the box. She didn't want anyone to know what was happening, because that is the way it was always done. Except I don't think any of this would have happened if she'd just told everyone what they would eventually learn anyway. A small community millions of miles from home is not the place for secrets."

She thought of how few people knew she was transgender, of all the other secrets that everyone here likely kept, the skeletons in their closets that they had run all the way here from, and she had to come to the conclusion that Metzger was being naïve. Somewhere millions of miles from humanity was the perfect place for secrets. But she didn't say that. Leah suspected he had a point he needed to make.

"The truth needs to be known and dealt with. We cannot hide from it. So..." He gestured for her to take the PDA again. This time, she tentatively took it. She touched the button to bring up the screen, which immediately asked for the password. She was about to try something that seemed appropriately Metzger-like, probably 123456789 or 987654321 or even, heaven help her, PASSWORD. Before she could enter anything, though, he told her.

"The password is uH98%(pxRR#5."

She blinked at him, impressed, then put it in. Another prompt came up for a second password.

"And that one is?"

"Puppies. With a capital P."

She entered it. There was a file front and center, obviously the one she had been after all day. Leah took a deep breath before opening it.

25

At 7:38 p.m. Rothschild Standard Time, every intercom, speaker, phone, and PDA in the three Martian colonies came alive with an announcement. Except for some of the people of Kurtis and Rochelle who had never had many dealings with him, everyone was surprised not only to hear Hans Metzger's voice, speaking in French so the largest number of people would understand him, but also that he sounded more confident and determined than they'd ever heard him before. Part of that was because he was reading off a speech that Leah Hartnup had helped him prepare, and part of that was because she was standing beside him in Westin's former office as he spoke, squeezing his shoulder and silently offering support that she didn't feel qualified to give at this moment.

"Attention people of the three colonies of Mars. This is Hans Metzger, deputy director of mining colony Miranda. There may be many of you who know by now why I am addressing you all, while many of you may not."

In the Miranda habitat wing, Jeanette Weasel stopped the handjob she'd been giving rover pilot Vladimir Petrenko and listened. He protested for a moment but Weasel gave him a dirty look and he stopped.

"Just short of one hour ago, an unknown assailant attacked two people, Director Tasha Westin and Annabeth Crick. While Annabeth Crick is currently in a coma, it is with great remorse that I must announce that Director Westin is dead."

In the commons wing Priyanka Kapoor, Nadeem Aslam, and Faisal Murad had just finished their movie. Neither Aslam nor Murad spoke French, so Kapoor had to translate for them. She found each word out of her mouth harder than the last.

"While we are still working to determine the exact nature and reason of the attack, I assure everyone that the murderer will be caught, given a fair hearing, and if found guilty punished according to the law."

Having just got back to his apartment, Mikhail Svensson sat on the floor of his kitchenette and stared longingly into his now empty mini refrigerator. There wasn't any amount of money he wouldn't give for an egg about now. He heard all Metzger's words but didn't bother paying attention to them.

"A memorial for the director will be arranged when possible. I ask that everyone keep both the director and Miss Crick in your thoughts and prayers, regardless of which deity you may believe in."

Takibana Ishikawa stood over Westin's body in the clinic, knowing his investigation into her murder needed to begin sooner rather than later and that every moment wasted was the one that might allow the killer to get away with it. Yet he couldn't force himself to move, instead staring down at the towel someone had placed over his lover's face. He didn't cry. He'd already done all the crying he intended to do.

"But there is something far more important that must be discussed. As horrific as this evening's events at Miranda have been, they pale in comparison to what I must tell you next."

In a small cell in Kurtis that had been temporarily transformed into a living space, Suzie Kleinstock sat on a cot with her legs hugged tight to her chest, nervously tracing patterns over the black skin of her arms. She already knew what Metzger was about to say. She had known it before nearly everyone else, and she'd been near-catatonic with the knowledge ever since she'd been roughly thrown into the transport rover and taken here.

"A pandemic has been unleashed on Earth. A virus known as Bratsk that seems to have originated in Siberia has broken out and spread all across the planet. Every indication is that the virus works quickly, is airborne, and has a hundred-percent fatality rate."

In his sleeping quarters no larger than a closet, Sandeep "Dip" Benegal sat on the edge of his bed and listened in absolute horror. The message from this morning slowly started to make more sense. He whispered silent prayers to his gods, but for the first time he wondered if Mars was too far away for them to hear.

"Our last contact with Earth was earlier in the day. We have repeatedly tried to reestablish contact with the Rothschild Syndicate, but we are not receiving any response. Attempts to contact other agencies, corporations, or governments have been similarly ineffective."

In Rochelle, Anna Gromov sat at her desk in her office. She'd cried earlier but thought she was done for now. On top of the scattered papers of her desk she had a bottle of booze, purchased about twenty sols ago from Jeanette Weasel. It would probably be one of the last such bottles seen on Mars. Against stereotype, though, it wasn't Russian vodka. It was tequila, and Gromov had drunk over half the bottle in just the last ten minutes. Her stomach felt like it was about to explode, and she got the impression she was about to learn what low-gravity vomit looked like.

"Although we intend to continue trying to contact home and hope that the situation is not as dire as we believe, we must be prepared and ready for the possibility that this is not a mistake or an issue that can be resolved. We must consider the possibility that the Rothschild colonies are permanently cut off from planet Earth."

Miner Jay Davis, as he was known on Mars, worked restlessly on a weight machine in the exercise room. He had the entire room to himself. Everyone else had vacated to be with people they cared about as they heard the news. Davis didn't have anyone, though. No friends, no loved ones, no one who even knew his real name or purpose on this planet. If what Metzger said was correct, then the people who'd put him here were either dead or dying. He'd never felt more alone, and he pushed his body harder against the machine, trying to replace one pain with another.

"It is imperative that no one panic in this our hour of greatest need. The survival of each and every person on the planet depends on the actions and deeds of everyone else around them. We must work together or else face horrible consequences to all of us."

Darlene Anguitine, head of media relations, sat alone in her office, listening quietly to every word Metzger said. She did not frown, cry, wrinkle her brow in worry, smile, laugh, sigh, or any other reaction that most people would think might be merited in this situation. She simply listened, thought, and planned.

"Tomorrow morning at 8:00 a.m. Rothschild standard time, there will be a meeting in the Miranda conference room. There will be a telepresence connection with the Kurtis and Rochelle meeting rooms. Anyone and everyone is encouraged to attend. We will discuss what will happen from here and how we will proceed."

Throughout all three colonies, couples huddled close together. The Lipschitzes hugged in their clinic apartment. Miranda head cook Wallace Barkley and his assistant Mina Alvarez held hands in the kitchen. In Rochelle, Chanelle and Michael Mkanda, who had been in the middle of some play involving a makeshift cat-o-ninetails when Metzger had started, were now curled up together on their bed in a much more vanilla show of support and affection. Even custodian David Bechdel, who had been paying for an hour with Karen Sulford, stroked her gently as she shivered at every word.

For the first time in his speech, Metzger faltered. He felt there had to be more he could say or do. He looked over at Leah Hartnup, but she had a faraway look in her eyes that told him she wouldn't be giving him more help anytime soon. As much as he hated to leave it at that, there was nothing else to say. Words wouldn't do much more. The only thing that remained to the people of Mars was to survive.

The intercoms abruptly switched off. Soon after the sun set on Poynting Crater, and a long night began.

Cast of Characters:

Miranda Colony (58 people):

Annabeth Crick- American, "working girl"

Leah Hartnup- Welsh, transgender (not public knowledge), computers and electronics

Sandeep "Dip" Benegal- Indian, miner

Mikhail Svensson- Swedish, production manager

Jeanette Weasel- "working girl," black market

Wallace Barkley- African American, head cook

Mina Alvarez- Mexican, assistant cook

Dr. Isaac Lipschitz- Austrian Jew, medical doctor

Clara Lipschitz- Austrian Jew, nurse and medic

Anil Khan- Indian, miner

William York- British, miner, Christian pastor

Ravi Gavankar- Indian, miner, Hindu pujari

Parviz Hosseini- Afghani, miner

Tasha Westin- American, bisexual, Chief Director of Miranda

Karen Sulford- "working girl"

Dr. Mario Pereira- Brazilian, chief science advisor

Suzie Kleinstock- Canadian, computers and programming

Takibana Ishikawa - Japanese, chief of security

Aishwarya Simmons- Indian, deputy chief of security

Matsumoto Haruma - Japanese, security

Monique Kristfal- British, security

Bindi Gruber- Australian, security

Dr. Martin Ruiz- Brazilian, biologist

Schwartzmann- meteorologist

Roy Osbourne- American, miner

Arne Bergland- Swedish, gay, miner

Dev Jaffrey- Indian, gay, miner, informal head of mining crew

Darlene Anguitine- media relations

Jay Davis - American, miner

Martin Freelis- British, water management

Hans Metzger- German, Deputy Colony Director of Miranda

David Bechdel- American, head custodian

Priyanka Kapoor- Indian, water plant worker

Nadeem Aslam- Pakistani, tool and die maker

Faisal Murad- Pakistani, tool and die maker
Max Perrish- deceased, former miner, real name Louis Maxwell Murphy
Dr. Bassinger- American, Miranda psychologist
Vladimir Petrenko- Ukrainian, supply rover pilot

Kurtis Colony (50 people):
Peter Renner- American, gay, Deputy Colony Director of Kurtis

Rochelle Colony (48 people):
Anna Gromov- Russian, Deputy Colony Director of Rochelle
Chanelle Mkanda- geologist
Michael Mkanda- custodian

People on Earth:
Mallika- Dip's sister
Sendhil- Dip's brother-in-law
Rochelle Rothschild- CEO of the Rothschild Syndicate
Kurtis Rothschild- board member of the Rothschild Syndicate
Miranda Rothschild- board member of the Rothschild Syndicate

www.ingramcontent.com/pod-product-compliance
Lightning Source LLC
Chambersburg PA
CBHW032209170626
46808CB00006B/2393